THE ODD ADVENTURES OF EMILY AND STEVEN

Written by E. S. Edmunds
Artwork by S. D. Thomas

Wandering Pen Publishing, West Chicago, IL
ISBN-10: 0692755233
ISBN-13: 978-0692755235
Library of Congress Control Number: 2016912303

Typography by S. D. Thomas

First Edition

For Mom and Dad, who saved me from laziness
and believed in me enough to support me.

−E.S. Edmunds

Dear Reader,

Hello! Pleased to meet you. If I could I'd give you a nice handshake, but considering I'm here and you're all the way over there, it is rather impossible at the moment. Still, consider your hand shaken nonetheless.

Now that all that's over with, let me just say that you're really fortunate to have come across this book. You see, the occurrences within these pages were too fantastic not to record, and therefore I found it extremely important to make sure they were all written down and properly documented. Soon you'll find yourself in a completely different world with all sorts of wonderful—ah, I'd better stop myself there. I'd hate to ruin the story. After all, what sort of adventure would it be if I told you all about it now? I mean, it would still be exciting, of course, but the suspense of it all would disappear and since the good parts would have been revealed now, you'd more than likely leave this book on your shelf, forgetting about it. Then, years later you'd find it again and only think of how that silly author gave away their entire story right on the first page. So! I won't do that. I won't even say another word about the story. Instead, I will leave you with a nice, solid bit of advice. Advice is always good, isn't it? Now, I must tell you that this is a precious piece of advice, so if you need to take a moment to prepare for it, please do so now.

Are you ready?

Oh, not yet?

Okay, well, go ahead and read the next sentence whenever you feel fully prepared. I'll just be here waiting.

Ready now? Good!

My most valuable piece of advice is this:

Turn the page and start reading.

—E.S. Edmunds

THE ODD ADVENTURES OF EMILY AND STEVEN

Through the Violet Light

One

THE FLOWER INCIDENT

OUR STORY (SOMEWHAT) BEGINS in a dull town by a Green Sea where everything is typical and boring. In this town, there is nothing interesting to see and no grand places to explore, and all of the people that live there look the same (which has resulted in many cases of mistaken identity by some children, who can never seem to tell their own parents apart from other parents). If you decided to take a stroll around the dull town by the Green Sea, it is likely that you would find yourself incredibly bored before you even started. Even though the buildings were bright and the sea was nearby, it could only cause feelings of sadness for one certain family. This family (who went by the last name, Pine) consisted of three people: one father, one mother, and their eleven-year-old daughter named Emily. You see, they were different from anyone that lived there, and because of this, they found themselves mocked and teased regularly. People looked at Mrs. Pine in a funny way, because she wore clothes of many different colors, while all of the other mothers wore nothing but white. Mr. Pine also got an equal dose of laughs because he wore big dark glasses, while all of the other fathers had perfect vision. Even though people in the town teased and mocked them, Mr. and Mrs. Pine found no reason to change because they realized that only ugly minds are good at teasing.

In the dull town by the Green Sea, no one painted, or wrote, or composed symphonies. Even though everyone knew that such wonderful things existed, they chose not to have any interest in them because they believed that such pursuits would only be a waste of their time. Because of this lack of interest, all of the adults worked either in dreary cramped offices, or in big gloomy factories. Mr. and Mrs. Pine had no choice but to work in a big gloomy factory where they spent all day gluing plastic covers (most literally known as 'aglets') on the ends of shoelaces. This job was horribly ordinary, and they despised it very much.

Now, you are probably wondering about Emily. To be honest, there is not much to say about Emily, because her story has not quite started yet (but all of this will change, as you will soon find out). A few things about her are worth mentioning now, though. First, she constantly found herself dreaming of adventure. Second, she was terribly shy. (To illustrate, she would shake like an autumn leaf whenever she had to speak to someone new, and this never failed to embarrass her.) Finally, she had long shiny black hair and big green eyes that always looked lonely and sad, which matched her personality. You see, like her parents, Emily was also different. Even though she was aware of this fact, she couldn't seem to figure out exactly what *made* her different. All the boys and girls in town ignored her, and when she was not building card houses with her father, or studying about plants with her mother, she was alone. Some days, if she felt agonizingly bored (it *is* a well-known fact that bored people experience a measure of pain), Emily would do one of her favorite things, which happened to be the unusual habit of spying on her neighbors as they walked mechanically in their backyard. This never gave her the excitement she wanted, but she still watched intently, hoping that they would do something out of the ordinary or dramatic. Of course, they never did, and they probably never would. In the end, Emily only wanted a bit of excitement, and most of the time, she was terrified that she would never find it. All of this began to change, though, on one warm summer weekend when Mrs. Pine woke up before the sun, and started to plant a garden. She spent all day in her backyard, surrounding herself with tulips, pinks, and daisies. The colors did not match, but they looked lovely together anyway. Mrs. Pine found so much happiness from her backyard garden, that she decided to plant flowers in her front yard, too. So, until the late hours of the night, she planted and planted until she had no more flowers left. The next morning, she woke up excitedly, only to find that all of her flowers were gone! On the front door, there was a lengthy note, and the first part of it said something like this:

"It has been observed that you have planted an outrageously colorful garden all around your home. This is unacceptable, as the colors of the flowers do not match the crisp white color of the houses. In order to maintain the clean, organized appearance of our neighborhood, we took it upon ourselves to remove all of the flowers. If such an incident happens again, we expect you to pay a fine..."

You see, Mrs. Pine found herself simply heartbroken over the fact that everyone in the dull town by the Green Sea viewed her flowers as a nuisance. For weeks and weeks after this incident, neighbors could only glance at the Pine family and scrunch up their faces. The children of the town laughed whenever they saw Emily walk down the sidewalks. How dreadful and unfair! This horrid treatment mainly cast a dark cloud upon Emily, which resulted in long days spent inside the house with the blinds shut. If the flower incident taught the Pine family anything, it was this: sometimes, bad things need to happen in order for good things to begin. The dull town by the Green Sea was no place for them to live. Why should they have to live in a place where they must ignore the things they enjoy? This was a question Mr. and Mrs. Pine asked themselves regularly. They kept on asking until they found an answer:

MOVE.

LEAVE.

ESCAPE.

These three words kept repeating in their minds. In the end, they believed that there was nothing better for them to do but heed those words, and move far away to a place called Wallowing Oaks and never look back.

Two

THE ESCAPE

On moving day, the clock ticked slower than ever, almost as if it were trying to prevent the Pine family from leaving. Emily, who normally held her patience well, found herself walking back and forth in the empty living room anxiously. She had no desire to take a final stroll around her old house, because frankly, she did not want to remember it. Instead, she tried to replace the images of her old house with the excitement of the new one. The only thing Emily knew about her new home was that it sat in a well-wooded neighborhood. Whenever her parents tried to describe what color the doors were, or how tall the ceilings stood, she would explain that she had never been surprised by anything before, and she wanted to know what it was like. Sometimes late at night, she would sneakily eavesdrop on her parents as they spoke of Wallowing Oaks. From her eavesdrops, she learned that Wallowing Oaks has three gardens, one amusement park, and two libraries. Something ordinary to many was a treasure chest of excitement to Emily, who had never strolled through gardens, or walked down old dusty hallways surrounded by books. She daydreamed of these places daily, and at nighttime before she fell asleep, they would be the only things on her mind.

The Pine family escaped the dull town by the Green Sea after breakfast, and found themselves in Wallowing Oaks before dinner. It was not difficult to realize when they got there, because as soon as they arrived, a big bold sign greeted them:

WELCOME TO WALLOWING OAKS!
We know that you'll be pleased.

The sign burst with colors. Around the words, there were trees, and birds, and houses painted. Yes, it was quite lovely indeed. An electric-like shock came over Emily when she saw the people that lived in Wallowing Oaks, because no one looked the same. Some people wore nothing but black, and others walked with a dance in their step. All of the children walked contently alongside their mothers or fathers, and they did not have to worry about misplacing their own parents amongst the others.

The Pine family traveled down a few different streets until they reached Windsong Lane, the street they would now live on. From the very start of the street, all of the houses were different colors and styles, and all of the yards had fantastic gardens. (None of the flowers in these gardens matched, which was quite a relief to Mrs. Pine, as you can imagine.) From the sidewalks, there was a symphony of sounds. The laughter of children on one side, the jovial sound of dinner plates and silverware clacking through kitchen windows, and the sound of opera music from a nearby attic. The street was alive, and for the very first time in her life, Emily wondered if she was living in a dream.

Before Emily saw the new home, Mr. and Mrs. Pine made sure that she closed her eyes (they did want her to be surprised, after all). Once she closed her eyes, they both took her by the hand and led her to the yard, and Emily anxiously waited, trying her best not to peek until her parents said it was time. "Okay, Emily. You can open your eyes now," whispered Mrs.

Pine, hardly able to contain her own excitement.

Emily opened her big, green eyes swiftly, and the first thing that she saw was a tall wooden door with a small red bird painted on the front. Her eyes soon adjusted, and she found herself gazing at the house in its entirety. "So, what do you think, my dear girl?" asked Mr. Pine.

"Oh, it's marvelous," said Emily in a dreamy sigh. She did not say much about the house, because she could not figure out the right words to express how much she loved it. Even though she thought herself to be quite silly, the first thing the house made her think of was a cake, which was actually a spot-on observation, because the house happened to be designed by a cake baker. To explain, the bricks were vanilla white, and the roof was a sugary shade of pink. There had also been reports that in the past, some people would see it from a distance and assume that it was an incredibly large cake, and when they asked for the recipe, they would find themselves with nothing but a long list of how to build a house.

The inside of the house did not resemble any sort of dessert, but it was fantastic anyway. The setting sun gleamed through the windows and onto the floors creating a parade of shadows. A mysterious and alluring staircase also greeted them, and

Emily could not help but sneak upstairs to determine which room she wanted. As she crept up the steps, she prepared herself for what she expected to be a horribly difficult decision. The first room on the right was far too big, and she concluded that it was not the correct room for her (she wanted to be reasonable, after all). The first thing she saw in the second room was a tall window that looked into the neighbor's backyard. If you have a good memory, you will recall that spying on neighbors was one of Emily's favorite things to do, and since this room had the perfect equipment for doing so, she decided that this was the room for her.

Now, since the house had been empty for a while, there happened to be a collection of dust on the windowsills, and Emily decided to open the window. After doing so, she sat down on the wooden floor and gazed at her new room. As she gazed, she imagined waking up each morning, seeing the yellow walls, and feeling happy. She gazed and gazed and gazed at her room, allowing the very sight of it to stay fixed in her mind because she did not want to forget her first impressions of it. Suddenly, though, a voice coming from outside interrupted her, and it spoke with elegance:

"*Little sleeveless coat and me,*
Walking under the clouds and trees,

Drinking tea, eating cake,
Sleeveless coat and I feel great.
Up and down the sidewalks wide
The little sleeveless coat and I stride–"

As this voice spoke more and more, Emily ran to her window, only to find a young boy with hair of white gold standing outside. He held a bright white piece of paper and seemed to be reciting some sort of poem to his toy animals in the backyard. *I suppose he is my neighbor,* Emily whispered to herself as she stared at him intently.

"—But then came winter cold and dim!

The little sleeveless coat had to stay in!

It made me very sad to see it wait!

For winter to pass and spring to elate!"

With each passing sentence, his voice gained more volume and feeling. The way he spoke was a bit strange to Emily because never in her life had she heard someone speak that way before.

"What a *PECULIAR* boy!" she yelled (forgetting that her

window was wide open).

As soon as the words left her mouth, the boy jumped in shock and, for a minute or two, looked around nervously for a visitor. "Excuse me, is someone there?" he asked anxiously.

To Emily, the sky got closer, the houses grew smaller, and the treetops tickled her nose: she did not know how to respond. (If you have ever had the misfortune of not knowing how to respond to someone, you may recall feeling incredibly large to the point where it seems like the entire world is watching you and waiting for you to speak.) Even though her voice was shaky, she replied to the boy, "Oh, please forgive me," she cried. "I'm so sorry. I just moved here, and I heard you speaking and…"

"Say no more. Since you're up there, and I'm down here, I can't help but ask you to come down so I can introduce myself to you properly. You must excuse me; I've never been good with heights."

To put things lightly, Emily was terrified to meet her neighbor after declaring him peculiar. Still, she followed the path to his backyard garden, and for a moment, she stood and stared at him from the green leafy entryway. From a distance, he looked to be her age. He wore a pale blue summer suit, and his complexion was pasty. There was a pensive expression painted upon his face, and despite his age, he looked as if he were the wisest person alive. Emily (who, at this point, found herself fascinated by her neighbor) now realized that she was standing in the entryway so long, only to avoid speaking to him. Once she stepped next to a bed of chrysanthemums, though, the boy turned his head in enchantment,

"You must be Emily," he said, sounding more pleasant than expected. "My name is Steven, but before I say anything else, I must let you know that I very much dislike the name Steven, and I never would have chosen it for myself."

"It's nice to meet you, Steven. How do you know my name?" asked Emily, unable to look her neighbor in the eye.

"My grandmother and your mother were speaking with each other a few minutes ago. Your mother mentioned that she has a daughter named Emily and I figured she was speaking of you. That is, unless she has two daughters named Emily, which is highly unlikely."

"I see. I really hope that I didn't offend you earlier."

"Why would you have offended me? Being called peculiar is very much a compliment. It lets me know that I am not like anyone else, which is a wonderful way to be, don't you agree? Anyway, welcome to Wallowing Oaks. I'm sure you will enjoy it."

"Thank you, Steven. I only hope it is a bit different than the dull town by the Green Sea."

"Is that so? Why was the town by the Green Sea so dull?"

"Oh, it was gray and lonely. There was no art or flowers, or trees, or music. I hated it."

Steven looked at Emily with pity, "Was *anything* about it interesting?" he asked.

"Not even a bit. I would tell you more about it, but there is nothing left to say," sighed Emily.

In realizing that Emily did not want to talk about the dull town by the Green Sea anymore, Steven decided to speak about himself for a moment, "You may wonder what I was talking about when you were spying on me earlier," he said, looking up to the orange evening sky. "I like to write, and make art with words. Did you know that words are no different from paints and brushes? It's true," he continued.

His words introduced Emily to unfamiliar thoughts, and once again, she did not know how to respond, and found that it was easiest to reply with one simple word, "How?"

"Well, instead of saying that the sky is orange, you could say that it is ablaze with the sun's fire. Things like this paint pictures in your mind, you see."

Before Steven could say anything else, Emily's father called her from the window and asked her to help him unpack. This marked the end of Emily's first conversation with her new neighbor, and like any worthwhile conversation, it left her with fantastic new thoughts and ideas.

Three

THE HOLLOW TREE

As the evening progressed, a storm travelled through town, and Emily spent the rest of the rainy evening helping her parents unpack. By the time they finished, her clothing hung perfectly in a blue wardrobe, lights illuminated the yellow walls, and her bed sat neatly in the corner. For a little while, she rested on her floor, looking up at the ceiling and playing with the shadows. She made shapes of elephants and lions, and sometimes, she would shake her hands in attempt to make it look as if they were speaking to each other. Once she was quite finished with this, she decided to walk across her floor, strictly for the purpose of trying to find the spots with the most creaks. By the time she had covered each square inch of the floor, she concluded that there were three creaky spots, and marked them with rugs so she would not accidentally step on them at nighttime. After a little while, she peeked out her window and thought about Steven, which made her feel curious. These feelings of curiosity were quite new to Emily, who had never wondered about someone so much in her life, especially coming from the dull town by the Green Sea, where she had no one to wonder about. Many times in life, we must face the odd occurrence of thinking about someone we do not know very well, and imagining what their life must be like. We may imagine them owning a vast piano collection, or living in a secret castle. Emily imagined Steven as a sort of wanderer that never settled for one particular place. She pictured him wandering through meadows, and forests, and mountains. The more she thought about it, the more she wondered if he really did do such things. These thoughts eventually caused her to inhale a yawn, and exhale it slowly. Even though her mind was wide awake, her eyes could not stay open for another second, and she fell asleep peacefully, free from any worry of tomorrow's boredom.

In the midst of her slumber, the sound of footsteps outside woke her up, and when she opened her eyes, she found that a glistening violet light illuminated her entire room. As she sat up in her bed staring at it, she wondered if she was only dreaming (until she reasoned with herself that it simply must be real, or she would not be wondering if it were a dream). Curiosity struck again. It was the same curiosity that made her wonder so intently about Steven and Wallowing Oaks. This particular type of curiosity overcame her terribly quickly, and she could not stop herself from springing up out of bed and running to the window.

Once a bit of the fog cleared, she found that the violet light came from the hollow tree in her neighbor's backyard. Gradually the light faded, revealing the gray silhouette of what looked to be Steven standing alone in front of the tree with his hand resting on the edge of its hollow. Emily's mind was still a bit hazy from just waking up, and naturally, she wasn't thinking correctly. *Well, if that is Steven,* she thought, *he seems to be quite preoccupied with whatever strange thing he's doing, and it would be too silly to try to ask him about that peculiar type of tree right now.*

As Emily kept staring down at the tree, Steven looked straight up into her window and tilted his head to the side. At that very moment, Emily remembered that she fell asleep with her window wide open, and in the darkness of midnight, he could vaguely see her sticking her head outside. Like a bolt of

31

lightning, she slammed her window shut and stumbled into her bed again, and instead of dwelling on her embarrassment, she fell back asleep and dreamt of the strange violet light that shined from the hollow tree.

Four

STEVEN'S SECRET

The second Emily woke up, the first thing on her mind was, of course, the glowing violet light and the silhouette of Steven in front of it. No matter what she did, she could not help but think of those two peculiar things. As she ate her breakfast, she tried to distinguish whether or not it was a dream, or if it was real. She tried to think of reasons why it could have been a dream, but in the end, she could not figure out how something so realistic could possibly be a figment of her imagination. As Emily continued to think, her mother came walking into the kitchen. "Good morning, Em!" she said. "The nice woman next door invited us over to her house this afternoon. Wasn't that nice?"

Emily nodded her head.

"I saw you speaking to her grandson yesterday," continued Mrs. Pine. "How did he turn out?"

"Well, his name is Steven, and he seems interesting."

"Good! Maybe you two will end up being great friends," said Mrs. Pine kindly before she went outside to plant flowers in her new mismatched garden.

Emily stood up from her chair and looked outside, letting the sunlight hit her face, *I don't think the violet light would have been this warm*, she thought. *It was too pale to be warm. But…could it have been a cold light? Can any light be cold, or is all light warm?* Her mind was now tied in knots, and with each thought, the knots grew tighter. Then, she borrowed her mother's binoculars and looked at the hollow tree from her bedroom window. Below the hollow, there were three small steps, and they looked rickety, as if they could break at any moment. *There must be a reason for those steps*, she concluded. *Maybe they are for tree climbing. But, why do the steps stop at the hollow?* By this time, the knots in her mind were so tight that her head ached. Still, she kept looking. The next thing she wanted to study was the hollow itself, so she kept adjusting the lenses of the binoculars until they magnified it perfectly. The inside of the hollow was dark, and there was nothing to see except a few leaves. The more she looked, though, she found something that caught her eye. *Is that cotton?* she wondered while staring at a white, fluffy object that was stashed in the corner. Before she could sit down and study it, her mother informed her that it was time to visit the neighbors. Suddenly, a strange nervousness befell her. You see, she had never been invited to someone's home before, and she didn't quite know how to react to it, except to feel nervous.

Emily rang the doorbell (rather hesitantly) and within seconds, Steven's grandmother greeted them.

"Oh, it's so nice to finally meet all of you! Please come in!" she said with a bright, cheery smile.

Her smile made Emily uneasy because, in the dull town by the Green Sea, the only time people smiled at her was when they thought her hair or dress looked funny. When a giggle didn't follow the grandmother's smile, though, Emily knew that the smile was sincere, and she finally felt at ease.

The house was full of things: old things, odd things, and most of all, dusty things. Many of these things were new to Emily. For example, old, wrinkled maps of the world covered the walls, and one of the rooms was full of nothing but books that were tightly packed on shelves as tall as the ceiling. If anything, the house was more like a library or museum. The grandmother led Emily and her parents into a bright, balmy sunroom with a table that was set with glasses of lemonade and plates of sugar cookies. From inside the sunroom, Emily could plainly see the hollow tree, and to her surprise, the fluffy white object was gone. "I do hope the lemonade isn't too tart for you, dears," cried the grandmother who, at her age, had a horribly difficult time distinguishing what tastes sweet and what tastes sour. "Please, sit down and make yourselves comfortable!" she continued.

So, the Pine family sat down in their seats and sipped their lemonade (which happened to be the tartest lemonade they had ever tasted), and enjoyed the company of their new neighbor. Emily tried to keep her table manners, but in all honesty, significant things consumed her mind, and she could not help but constantly glance at the hollow tree. In noticing this, the grandmother began to speak, "My husband's father planted that tree many years ago, and ever since I can remember, the hollow has been there. I'm sure there are many stories behind that tree, but since he went missing, they can never be told."

"Missing? Who went missing?" asked Emily.

"My husband went missing. He went missing without a trace when the children were young," the grandmother's voice became softer. "There is another time and place for this conversation, dear Emily. Now, Steven is in the backyard, I believe. Would you like to visit with him?"

Emily agreed, and as soon as she stepped outside, she found Steven sitting under the shade of the hollow tree with a glass of lemonade and a book about Mount Everest. "Hello, Steven. How are you doing today?" she asked.

"Oh, good afternoon, Emily. I'm quite well. How are you?" he replied, a bit startled by her sudden arrival.

"Well," she began, "I didn't get much sleep last night, because a strange violet light shined in my window. I'm still trying to figure out what it was. Would you have any idea?" After Emily asked this question, she regretted it. The look upon Steven's face was a look of sheer surprise, almost as if the secret of the light were a treasure that he tried to keep to himself. By this time, Emily's curiosity was unbearable until the boy spoke again.

"Emily, let me ask you a question: when you look at the fluffy white clouds amongst the vivid blue sky, what do you see?" he asked.

"All I see are clouds and nothing else."

Steven crossed his arms and looked straight up to the fluffy clouds, "Emily, Emily, Emily! How can you only see clouds when you could look at them with the power of imagination and turn them into anything? Do you want me to tell you what I see?" he continued. "I see a huge fluffy bed that's close enough for me to climb up onto and take a nap at noon. When I wake, I'll be greeted by the big, bright moon. Th-that's it! This will be my next poem! Excuse me, Emily, I must go inside and write all of this down. Maybe later, I can unveil my masterpiece."

Before Emily could reply, Steven ran inside, leaving her alone in front of the hollow tree— that odd hollow tree. *Oh, if only I could talk to this tree,* she said to herself. *I wonder if it would answer my questions.* At this point, Emily found herself terribly inquisitive over everything, and she had to sit down. Her mind constantly spun around with thoughts of that strange violet light. If you have ever found yourself burdened with thoughts that you simply could not get rid of, then there is a good chance that you know exactly what Emily was going through.

For most of the afternoon, Emily sat underneath the hollow tree, and wondered. She wondered how tall the tree was, and she wondered how it got its hollow. All of her wondering sped up the time, and soon enough, she saw Steven stroll into the backyard again. "Emily! Emily! I'm finished now. You must hear my new poem," he cried while briskly waving a wrinkled sheet of paper in the air. "You absolutely must stay in your seat while you listen to this poem!"

So, Emily continued to sit under the hollow tree and listened to the words that Steven would now speak:

"I could easily climb onto the clouds
And take a nap at noon
I'd lay there asleep in my content
And wake up to the moon.
He would invite me as his guest
To stay awake all night.
Kindly, I would accept
(And compliment his face so bright).

I'd meet his friends, the stars
And collect some of their dust
We'll dance around so happily
(And never really feel rushed).
Oh! What a fantastic time we'll have!
Our hearts will be full of glee,
And when I breeze back to my home
My friends in the sky will miss me!

I'll see them again, but not too soon
The clouds must be just right
For me to climb them, nap at noon
And meet my friends at night."

"So…what do you think?" he asked through a delighted smile.

"It's- it's amazing! I'm completely amazed!" exclaimed Emily.

"I knew you would be! See Emily, isn't it interesting to paint with words?"

"Yes! How do you come up with the stories and words?"

"Well, it's inspiration. Without inspiration, I would never be able to do anything!"

"Where do you find inspiration?" asked Emily.

Steven drew in a breath. "Well, I find inspiration through many things, Emily. There is one thing that inspires me the most, though."

Emily was captivated.

"Remember our conversation earlier, when you asked me about the violet light?" he asked.

"Oh! Yes, I do!" said Emily. By this time, she was nearly jumping out of her seat.

"Well," he began, "I was coming back from a secret world; a different world. It may sound silly at first, but it *is* a real place. It's called Alcovia. The violet light you saw was coming from this hollow tree. The hollow is the only way to get in…as far as I know. Oh, Emily, you would love it there. It's a place where all imagination comes to life."

Steven and Emily could only look at each other silently.

"I don't mind if you think I'm mad. In fact, I hope you think I'm a *bit* mad. I wouldn't be interesting otherwise," he continued.

Emily was lost for words again. If this did not trouble her enough, she now had to contemplate whether Steven was telling the truth or not. Never had she heard of Alcovia (or any secret world, for that matter). And how strange it was that the only way to get there was through a certain tree hollow! In fact, it was all so unusual that Emily could not help but ask Steven if he was joking.

"I don't see how this could be a lie. You saw the light, didn't you? Isn't that enough proof?" he asked sullenly. "If you still don't believe me, I can take you there," he added. By this time, Emily decided that she could not say no. It all sounded too interesting, and she hated to miss a chance to have the adventure she wanted, even if the very idea made her a bit nervous.

"I think I'd like to go with you. Will anyone know we're gone?" she asked.

"No one will know we're gone, because when we go to Alcovia, time in this world freezes. I must add that you're the only one who knows about Alcovia, and you mustn't tell anyone! Promise you won't?"

"Oh, I promise. When can we go?"

"I'll be right here waiting at exactly midnight, and you must make sure you wear your fanciest clothing."

"Why should I wear my fanciest clothing?"

"You'll see when we get there."

Now to Emily, it felt as though the world spun around in a thousand circles, and it made her feel terribly dizzy. *How could a secret world exist?* she thought to herself while staring at her clock. It was now fifteen minutes before midnight. A shimmering pink dress sat on the edge of her bed, and it was still wrapped up in tissue paper. She never had a chance to wear it in the dull town by the Green Sea, and hoped that it would look fancy enough. The hands on the clock quickly spun towards midnight, and before Emily left, she took a glance at herself in the mirror (she took the fancy dress rule seriously). Finally, under the star-covered sky, she followed the moonlit path to Steven's backyard, where he waited for her in anticipation.

"You're exactly one minute late! We must get going!" he said in an unusually loud whisper. With no words, Emily took his hand and up they climbed into the hollow tree that glowed in a glistening violet sparkle.

In this same moment, they inhaled the cool, misty air of Alcovia.

Five

WELCOME TO ALCOVIA

"Are you okay, Emily?" asked Steven as soon as he saw that Emily had landed onto the ground (to be quite truthful, when you arrive into a secret world, falling onto the ground when you arrive is rather common).

"I think so. Where exactly did we enter from?"

"Oh…from the sky. As far as I know, there is no other way to get here," said Steven as he gazed up.

The sky in Alcovia was astonishing. It had three moons and millions of stars that constantly moved about as though they were dancing. Even though the moons and stars were present, it was not quite nighttime. You see, in Alcovia, it was never daytime, and it was never nighttime. Instead, it was like the last few minutes of the day when the sun and moon meet to create bursts of violet and orange.

"Steven...how do we get back home?" asked Emily with a tremble of worry in her voice.

"I have a special whistle with me," replied Steven. "The clouds in Alcovia are much like pets, you know. For some unknown reason, they respond quite happily to the jangly sound of this particular whistle. If I use it, a cloud will come down for us and take us anywhere we please. Only one of these whistles exists, so if we lose it, we could be stuck here for a very long time."

"What if it gets lost?" asked Emily, hoping for a positive answer.

"I'm wearing it around my neck, and it has no possible way of getting lost. Please don't worry, Emily. A mind full of worries never does any good."

Knowing that the special whistle hung safely around Steven's neck did seem to get rid of Emily's worries, and finally, she could stare into the sky. Emily's first few glances of Alcovia caused her to recall the poem that Steven wrote, and she was now beginning to see just how Alcovia inspired him.

Emily continued to stare into the sky until her eyes hurt. When she looked down, a collection of trees and other sorts of nature greeted her eyes. From what she could tell, she and Steven were in the middle of a forest, and they stood on a path that stretched as far as the eye could see.

"I know where we're going now!" shouted Steven while folding his map and stuffing it in his pocket. "I think you're going to love it, and the trip there is rather lovely."

They walked and walked and walked down that long path, and Emily followed Steven closely.

The forest that they wandered through was, at first glance, just like any other normal forest. The leaves moved back and forth, as they would on any other tree, and they gave off a nice amount of shade. After a while, though, Emily gazed at the forest long enough, and saw something different. For some strange reason, though, she could not figure out what made it that way. You see, when the trees swayed, it sounded musical, and when the leaves moved about on their branches, it looked as if they were dancing. The combination of these things quickly reminded Steven of why he took Emily to Alcovia in the first place: "Emily! When the wind causes the trees to sway about, what do you hear? And when they move on their branches, what do you see?" he asked, while staring up at them adoringly.

"Well…I don't know, really."

"Just close your eyes and listen closely. What do you hear?"

As Emily closed her eyes and listened, she tried to figure out what the sound of swaying leaves could be comparable to. A crowd of people talking? No. Rain drops hitting the ground? Maybe, but not quite. Finally, it came to her: a symphony.

"It almost sounds as if the trees and leaves are playing instruments in a symphony," she said, hoping that Steven would accept her answer.

"I couldn't have thought of a better way to put it, Emily."

Emily pushed the hair from her face, and sighed with relief.

"Now that I think of it, I should have remembered to tell you to bring a notebook and ink-pen. I am almost certain that by the time we leave Alcovia, you will be thinking differently. It would be such a shame if you forgot all your thoughts. I forgot my notebook, but that shouldn't be a problem."

On and on they walked. The path didn't look longer, and it didn't look shorter. The length of it remained the same, no matter how many steps they took. As they walked, they spoke of all sorts of different things, and Emily could not help but ask Steven how he found Alcovia in the first place, to which he replied:

"I was in the attic one day, and I found a box. It was such a neat box, and I couldn't help but open it. Inside, I found two things: a book, and the whistle," his eyes got bigger. "The most interesting thing was the book. Oh, I wish I had it with me…"

"What was written in it?" asked Emily.

"Well, that's the most interesting part. On the first page, there was a sketch of the hollow tree. Beneath it were the words: *'the violet light at midnight, the violet light at midnight.'* After this, there were more pictures than words. A few of the pictures demonstrated how to use the whistle for calling clouds down. Most of the pictures are so faded that I can't figure out what they mean, and it looks like some pages were ripped out."

"Where is the notebook now?"

"It is still in the box in the attic. I tried to bring it here, but it won't fit through the hollow, it is rather long, you see."

"Where did it come from?" asked Emily (who, by this time, discovered her hidden talent for asking questions).

"I don't know. No one from Alcovia seems to know either. Sometimes, the wondering makes me want to run in circles until I'm numb from dizziness. Other times, I like the uncertainty. It makes each trip to this silly, fantastic place seem like an adventure."

After this, they were silent. They passed grassy fields and colorful gardens. The sky always stayed the same shade of purple, and Emily could never seem to figure out what time it was (and strangely enough, she didn't mind a bit). Finally, they saw a big building up the path. Steven walked towards it briskly, and each step was a firm indication of how many times he had been there in the past.

Six

THE MUSEUM OF ODDITIES

The building was quite old looking. It had a green roof and green pipes all around it, and the parts of it that were not blanketed in layers of ivy revealed that it was built with tan bricks. If you stood close enough to the building, you would find that in front of the steps, there was a silver sign that read:

ALCOVIA'S MUSEUM OF ODDITIES
Open to those who wonder/wander

The sign was quite clever, because if you happened to look

at it from the left, it said 'wonder' and if you looked at it from the right, it said 'wander'. Perhaps the most interesting thing was that, if you thought about it long enough, both words made perfect sense. Steven couldn't help but shake his head slowly with admiration whenever he saw that clever sign, "I'm wandering and you're wondering!" he laughed. "It seems to me like the museum is the best place for the both of us. How about we take a look, Emily?"

Emily agreed, and prepared herself for whatever happened to be on the other side of the doors. You see, she had always been more than uncomfortable around old things. The very thought of old, dusty artifacts from the past always seemed to take away a bit of feeling from her knees and head which, at times like this, was a terrible inconvenience. Steven took the first step inside the museum and Emily followed. No matter how lightly they walked, the floors screeched and creaked with every step, which in itself was an indication of the building's age. Aside from the squeakiness from the floorboards, the museum was as silent as the objects that resided in it.

The first thing they saw when they walked in was a sort of display. The top of it stated the word: 'MISSING' and underneath were two worn, colorless photos: one with a young boy and girl about Emily and Steven's age, and another with a bearded sailor standing next to his ship.

"How awful!" proclaimed Emily with a tremble in her words. "Who are they?"

The voice that replied was not Steven's, as Emily had expected, but a woman's (the co-museum keeper, to be exact).

"They, my dear child, are people who have been missing for a horribly long time. Viciously long, I might add. They were happy to live in Alcovia, but without any warning, they went missing. Never to be seen again. No, never. I do hate to think of where they might be now, so I just pretend that they're hiding somewhere. Somewhere safe where they are happy." The woman spoke so frighteningly fast that it seemed impossible for her rouged lips to keep up with her words. "What a viciously grim welcome I've given you! I despise being grim, but sometimes I can't help myself. I can't help myself at all."

"Poppy, there is no need to apologize," said Steven. "I would like you to meet Emily, she's my new neighbor."

Poppy's solemn face whipped into happiness. "A new neighbor means a new visitor! Steven, you are very kind to bring her here. Why, Emily, you must get a tour of the museum. You must get a tour indeed. My sister Pepper is lurking around somewhere, I should think. I should hope. She would love to give you a tour. Just love to. Wait here while I get her, won't you?"

Poppy hurried out of the room, leaving behind nothing but a quick puff of flowery-perfumed air.

The museum stayed silent in the moments that Emily and Steven waited for Pepper, and Emily's eyes gravitated like a magnet to that MISSING display. No matter how upsetting the display was, she had the horrible need to examine it further, and what she found was most interesting. You see, underneath each photo was a write-up describing each person, such as who they were and when they were last seen. Emily first found herself carefully reading the paragraph under the photo of the two children, which said:

FLORENCE AND LAURENCE
ARTISTIC CHILDREN OF THE BAKER:

As the twins of Alcovia's baker, Florence and Laurence were rarely seen without a fresh cookie in one hand and a paintbrush in the other. They were known all over for their polite nature and stunning painting skills.

These skills earned the children spots in this very museum for their artwork so all could enjoy it. They found inspiration from the weather, and were commonly seen gazing at the clouds, musing over what they could create next.

Shade Day (known as one of Alcovia's most treacherous days), was the last day anyone had seen Florence and Laurence. This particular day resulted in a disastrous windstorm. This windstorm is speculated as the cause of the children's disappearance, although the truth is still undisclosed.

After such a dreadful windstorm, their items, a paintbrush and sketchbook, were found outside the only hollowed-out tree in Alcovia. The sketchbook had a vague, early drawing of said tree with some sort of smoke (or perhaps, light) coming out of its hollow.

Any information on the children's whereabouts is scarce.

Emily's cheeks burned; still, curiosity convinced her to read about the sailor:

CAPTAIN CECIL, ADVENTROUS SAILOR:

Captain Cecil was not known to many, but only to a few. The reason for this was because of his sense of adventure. Despite being quite a sensible captain, he was almost always sailing on Alcovia's seas, rarely making an *appearance on land. Those who knew him well compared him to the sea itself: Calm when he wanted to be, and stormily adventurous the rest of the time. He described the sea as his home and he enjoyed diving to the bottom of it to discover new types of seashells. His discoveries are on display in the museum today.*

His two sons, Silas and Elliott, were the last to see him in the early morning hours of Shade Day before taking off on a weeklong sailing trip. On this particular Shade Day, there was a ruinous windstorm, which is thought to be the reason for his disappearance. The sails of his ship washed up on the seashore a month after he disappeared. He is suspected to have had a passenger with him, but the identity of this person is unknown.

Information on Captain Cecil's whereabouts has yet to be discovered.

The museum was no longer silent to Emily, whose mind was filling up with thoughts of how she hoped to find an answer. She was not afraid after reading about the missing people, but instead, the words left her uneasy. She could not imagine mere winds being powerful enough to cause people to go missing; still, she thought it would be best to conclude that any bizarre thing could happen in a place like Alcovia. As Emily studied the faces in the photos, a soft voice began to speak. "They both disappeared on the same day...there has not been a windstorm since." This voice came from Pepper, the other museum keeper. She was only a hair taller than Emily (who was already two inches short for her age), and when she stood next to her sister she looked like a child, even though she was the oldest of the two.

"Do you know where they went?" Emily asked.

Pepper shrugged her shoulders and frowned.

"This is Steven's neighbor," exclaimed Poppy to her sister (hoping to brighten up such a dour conversation). "I seem to have forgotten her name already, how awful of me. It's frightening how one's manners can disappear for a moment."

"Her name is Emily," said Steven.

"Oh, that's a stunning name. I believe that if the warm summer breeze had a name, it would be called Emily." Pepper said, in her gentle tone of voice.

Emily did not have the faintest idea of how to respond. She had never received such a fascinating compliment, and wanted her answer to sound equally as interesting. Before she could answer, though, Pepper spoke again, "I imagine you and Steven have other places to be, don't you? Well, perhaps we should begin our tour at this moment! I think you'll quite enjoy it, Emily. And, I know you've been in the museum many times, Steven, but the more times the better! So, let's proceed!"

Emily and Steven did as Pepper said and followed her down a dark hallway to a room that held the paintings of Florence and Laurence. Despite their importance, they were not the first things that Pepper pointed out. She first walked to an open case next to a large window that held many violet glowing flowers.

"These flowers are quite terribly important. They are glowing flowers that indicate the weather. You see, since these flowers are now violet, we know that the weather is just lovely. If they were blue, that would mean rain and storms were on the way. And, if they were gray and glowing once per second, this would mean that a grave windstorm was on its way."

"What do they look like when snow is coming?" asked Emily.

"Oh, sadly these flowers don't tell us whether or not it will snow. I believe it is because they like to make sure we are surprised occasionally. Snow is a wonderful surprise, you must admit."

"Are these flowers all over Alcovia?" Emily could not keep herself from asking questions, which made Pepper rather happy, because there was nothing she enjoyed more than answering them.

"Ah, that is a wonderful question, Emily. No. You cannot find them everywhere, which is bothersome to say the least. They are mainly found around the mountains and forests. They cannot survive by the sea. I believe they find the taste of salty air despicable."

Emily stared at the flowers until her eyes filled to the brim with astonishment. They were so fascinating to her, and she wished that all flowers glowed in the same way (that is, until she told herself that if all flowers did glow, their glow would not be quite as special anymore).

After admiring the flowers, Pepper began to draw attention to the colorful, well-lit wall that held all of Florence and Laurence's paintings.

"These paintings belonged to the twins that you read about earlier," Pepper said in a shivery voice (her voice always sounded quite shivery when there was something important to say).

There were exactly five paintings on the wall, and each of them sat in fancily-carved frames. All of the paintings focused on the same thing: a goldfish. "This particular collection is called 'The Escalation of a Goldfish' or, 'How Large a Goldfish Can Grow.'" (Most of the twins' works of art had two titles, which resulted from never being able to agree peacefully on just one.) "The subject of this collection focuses on the way goldfish can grow if you leave them in a big pool of water," Pepper explained.

In the first painting, the goldfish was barely visible. To see it, you had to stand very close, or open your eyes widely. No matter how small the goldfish was, it must have grown up quickly, because in the fourth painting, there was barely any room left around it! Even though each painting was fascinating, Emily found her eyes particularly attached to the last one. From what she saw, it looked as if the goldfish was inside some sort of dark cave. Its cheerful, sunny face was the only thing that seemed to be visible, because there was a large water stain near the middle of the canvas.

"Does this painting have a special story?" Emily asked Pepper.

"All paintings have special stories, and the story behind this one is extra special," Pepper cleared her throat. "Whenever the waves in the sea were calm, Florence and Laurence would take the goldfish for a ride on the sea. One day, the goldfish caught sight of a cave blanketed in diamonds and swam to it. Once it was inside, it refused to leave! As far as I know, it is still there today."

"How did Florence and Laurence get home?" asked Emily.

"They swam, of course! That is, as soon as they finished painting their goldfish in its new home. How they managed to paint in the middle of the sea and not get their canvas completely drenched, I'll never know."

As much as she enjoyed seeing the paintings of such a fantastic goldfish, Emily became rather tired of it and turned her attention to something new. The first thing that caught her eye was a sketch of the only hollow tree in Alcovia (which happened to be the same one mentioned on the 'MISSING' sign). The outlines of the tree were faded and the paper was stained and worn. Its corners were torn and wrinkled. If anything, the battered condition of it was a telltale sign of all that it had been through.

Pepper noticed Emily staring at the sketch, and took it off

the wall while staring at it with questioning eyes, "Even though it appears that it has been battered by the wind," said Pepper, "it was found underneath a large rock that sat right next to the same exact tree that this drawing depicts. Isn't that strange?"

Emily kept staring at the gray smoke (or light) that came out of the hollow, and Pepper, in noticing this, became more vocal than ever.

"I cannot hold my thoughts in any longer!" she proclaimed, her voice at high volume. "I have a theory. Would you like to know what it is?"

Emily and Steven didn't have a chance to answer before she spoke again.

"I think that is a light coming from out of that tree, and I think that tree has something to do with the twins' disappearance and maybe even Captain Cecil's! Now, follow me!"

Once again, they did as Pepper said, and followed her to a different room where she took them to a case that held Captain Cecil's seashells. Without saying a word, Pepper opened the top of the case, and grabbed from out of it a seashell that was so black it looked as if it came from the night sky.

"This was found in Captain Cecil's seashell collection. A black seashell has never existed in Alcovia before this, which could only mean one thing: it is from another place. I believe, with a heavy heart, that Captain Cecil and the twins have disappeared to the same place. Just where that place is, I have no idea. Oh, if only I knew." The museum overflowed with a sort of odd silence. It was the type of silence that occurs when there are many questions to be asked, but nothing left to be said.

"I hope you don't think I'm too odd in my thinking," Pepper said, followed by a bit of laughter.

"All of the best people are odd in their thinking. Could you imagine how dreary it would be if everyone thought the same things?" said Steven in reply (he was always fond of those who felt as if they were odd in one way or another, partly because he knew he was rather odd himself).

Emily stood beside the seashell case, idly gazing inside.

"Oh Emily, I have probably frightened you to bits, you

poor dear! Could I get you a warm cup of tea to wash away your fear?" asked Pepper.

"I think I'll be okay, but thank you for such a nice offer," Emily was trying very hard to sound fearless.

"I imagine you have many places you need to be. I hope I haven't been keeping you here longer than you expected! I feel as if I have so much to discuss, but never enough words," cried Pepper.

"I *do* hate to say it, but we must get going. Emily and I have places that we must be," said Steven. "I do wish to continue our discussion soon, Pepper," he continued.

On their way out of the museum, Emily made sure to take one more look of the photos. Her reason for this was that, if she happened to come across any of the missing people, she would remember their faces plainly and could identify them.

"Before you two leave," said Pepper, "I want to give you something." she left the room for a moment, and came back with a tin that was small enough to fit into a pocket. "I don't know if this will give you any peace of mind," she whispered, "but I think you'll appreciate it anyway." She handed the box to Emily, who opened it with much haste. When she opened it, she found a small flower that glowed in the color of violet.

"If you keep the flower in this tin," said Pepper, "it will survive any weather. Just make sure not to open it by the sea, because if you do, it will fade away. It will be incredibly useful, especially if you feel the weather is getting dicey."

"Thank you! We'll take very good care of it!" promised Emily before storing it away in her pocket. The very idea of having that flower did seem to put her mind at ease to the point where she could calm down a bit.

"Oh, you're welcome, Emily. Now, be on your way! There is so much to see in the beautiful Alcovia! And, please don't forget to visit me again."

"We could never forget about you, Pepper," said Steven from the bottom of the steps.

After saying their goodbyes, Emily and Steven followed the path through the forest once again, and discussed all that they saw in the museum.

Seven

DINNER WITH A TREE

On their way to the next place, they found themselves confronted with a quartet of singing bluebirds. The birds did not fly, but instead they strolled along and whistled. Perhaps the most peculiar thing was that they were all dressed up in little blouses and wore hats that were actually flower petals (pink tulips, to be exact). Emily made sure not to get too close to them. You see, she enjoyed looking at them so much and she feared that if she got too close they would scatter away to the sky or tree branches.

"Could we follow them for a little while, Steven? I'd like to find out where they're going."

The bluebirds, in overhearing Emily, whistled their tune a little louder. They quite enjoyed having an audience. Emily and Steven followed the bluebirds down the path for a little while until they all gathered in a garden. It was no ordinary garden, though. This garden happened to look strikingly similar to Steven's backyard, and Emily noticed this almost immediately. "Steven, this looks just like your garden!" she exclaimed, focusing on the rosebushes and trees.

"I've thought the same thing many times." (Steven really had no idea why the garden looked almost exactly like his). "You're becoming very observant Emily, which is quite a useful way to be!"

Suddenly, Steven went on to study each flower carefully, taking in the scent of their petals and affectionately stroking their leaves.

"Do you know what the best thing about flowers is, Emily?" he asked with his nose against a daisy. "The best thing about flowers is that, even though they're living, they never do one disgusting thing. I think that's lovely, don't you?"

"Oh yes, I've never thought about it that way before," Emily said in a soft, dazed voice. Her voice always sounded this way after she had heard something particularly interesting.

"I wish more people were like flowers," Steven said in continuation. "Even the prettiest of roses wouldn't *think* of teasing weeds or wildflowers for their floppy leaves. If a beautiful rose can be kind, then I'm sure it's in the heart of every living thing to be the same way."

He stared at the flowers for a moment longer and then, in the gentlest way, plucked two tall yellow flowers from the ground and stuck them in his pocket - an action that left Emily slightly perplexed.

"Why did you do that?" she asked.

"Because simply *looking* at these flowers makes me happy and reminds me to be kind. I've found that if you fill your world with things that make you happy and remind you to be kind, your entire life will be meaningful."

As all of this was going on, the quartet of bluebirds still whistled their tune in the garden. Suddenly, though, their whistles sounded farther away. The farther they got, the quicker the chirps sounded. After realizing that the bluebirds had wandered away from the middle of the garden, Emily and Steven decided to look for them. They followed the sound of the chirps and finally found the bluebirds gathered in a darkened corner, just outside a forest, and they circled around what seemed to be a tree. If it *was* a tree, it was quite unrecognizable because many of its roots were sticking out from the ground and its branches had no more than a few leaves on them.

"I've never seen a tree stump in Alcovia before," said Steven, crouching down to get a better look (it was not as tall as most trees).

The bluebirds kept on chirping and jumping up and down from the branches. They seemed so excited over the tree and this caused both Emily and Steven to examine it a bit further. Steven was the first to get close to the tree and as soon as he did, he found that it had a hollow. It was full of leaves, and when Steven cleared the leaves away, he found that the hollow did not seem to lead anywhere. Both he and Emily knew that it could be the same tree that Pepper spoke of, but how could they know for sure?

"I know exactly who could tell us about this tree, and

funnily enough, I was going to take you to meet them anyway!" exclaimed Steven. "Now, I think we should probably be on our way. Please follow me, Emily!"

They continued walking into the forest. There was no path to lead their way, but only signs. As you have probably noticed, Alcovia was a place that took great advantage of the practical use of signs.

The first sign that they came across had a startling message:

YOU ARE NOW ENTERING THE FOREST
(HOME OF HUNGRY TREES)

The message was especially startling to Emily, who could only imagine trees that were hungry for whoever passed them. In fact, the sign upset her so much that she wondered whether the forest would be worth walking through. How terrible it would be if she and Steven came across a hungry tree, and it caught one of them for dinner! While walking through the forest, she found herself confronted by a nightmarish memory from many years ago. You see, in the dull town by the Green Sea, the trees didn't have many leaves, which meant that if your hair was long enough, and if the day was windy enough, your hair could easily get tangled in the branches. Emily had always kept her hair rather long, and one day, while walking side by side with her mother, a gust of wind blew her hair around until it got caught in a short tree. Emily's mother tried to untangle it, but after hours of unraveling, she decided that the only way to free Emily was to cut her long black hair. Naturally, such a startling experience would inspire anyone to have a faint fear of trees. Emily also figured that the hungry trees would be terribly vicious, and she wanted to make her opinion known to Steven, who continued to walk with great confidence.

"Steven, are you sure it's all right to continue?" she asked bashfully with her eyes fixed to the ground.

Unlike Emily, Steven did not have the slightest bit of worry, which was obvious by his cool manner.

"Emily," he said sincerely, "if it's the hungry trees that make you weary, you shouldn't worry. I have dealt with hundreds, maybe even thousands of hungry trees before. Trust me, we will be perfectly fine; now let's go!"

As soon as Steven turned around to continue walking, Emily scrunched up her face. Either she had been walking for too long, or hungriness was finally starting to catch up with her (hungriness *is* known to bring out the worst in even the kindest of people, you know).

On and on they walked. Emily only found herself gaining more curiosity with each step. She was determined not to let her curiosity disappear, so in an attempt to get more answers, she asked Steven a question about the hungry trees.

"Steven? Just where are the hungry trees? I keep on looking out for them so that I will be fully prepared to fight them if they catch me for their dinner."

"Oh Emily, I am so sorry! I was so excited to enter the forest that I forgot to tell you that the hungry trees aren't dangerous at all! They will want to eat their meals with you, and won't let you go until they're finished. You see, they're slow eaters, and the only reason you want to beware of them is because they're completely time consuming. I must say that the sign is somewhat misleading…"

"Oh, it definitely is!" Emily said. "Come to think of it, it would be very interesting to see one of these hungry trees sometime," she added.

"It's quite funny you should say so," said Steven. "I was just on my way to take you to meet one!"

"How exciting! But how can I make sure that I don't get caught as their guest?"

"Well, the tree that I am taking you to visit is a friend of mine. I simply wanted you to meet her. If we make no mention of hungriness, then she won't make us stay for dinner. But if one of us talks about food, she will most certainly make us stay as her dinner guests! And, most importantly, do *NOT* let your stomach growl!"

All of this talk of hungriness suddenly reminded Emily of how long it had been since she had eaten. As soon as the thought of food entered her mind, she tried to get rid of it. It was no use though, because she only found herself thinking about it more and more until, suddenly: ROAR! Her stomach growled (quite louder than usual) and in that same terrifying moment at least five tree branches stretched out towards her and Steven, grabbing their hands and leading them underneath their shade. There, they found themselves seated at a large table that was set with every sort of dish, cup, and utensil imaginable.

"Emily, don't you remember me telling you not to let them

hear your stomach growl?" Steven whispered.

"I do, but this is all so new to me, and I didn't know how to control it! I'm sorry."

Before Steven could reply to Emily, one of the trees with a beautiful, yet obscure face began to speak to them softly: "Why, hello Steven! What a pleasure it is to see you again. And who is this? Do you have a friend with you?"

"It's a pleasure to see you again as well, Tree," Steven said politely. "Yes, this is my friend Emily, and this is her first time here in Alcovia. I thought it was quite important to take her for a stroll through the forest."

"What a wonderful evening it is for a stroll! The both of you must be famished though! Thank goodness I just prepared dinner, and I have plenty to share with you," Tree said while she gently pushed their seats in closer to the table with her leafy branches.

Before Emily and Steven knew it, two plates of little dinner cakes came rolling down the tree-branch and onto their plates. In a slight state of confusion as to what she should do next, Emily looked to Steven, who began to eat, just as if this were a normal occurrence.

Emily could not begin to understand all of the odd things that were taking place in that moment.

"Steven, does this always happen?" she whispered.

"Yes, it does, actually. You should probably be eating now, or else Tree will think you don't like it, and she'll get upset. Believe me, we wouldn't want that!"

Emily took Steven's word and ate the food from her plate, and it was quite unlike anything she had eaten in her entire life. In fact, it tasted so delicious that she could not contain her thoughts about it.

"Tree, this is one of the best things I have ever eaten!" she yelled (with her cheeks still stuffed with food).

Tree's obscure face smiled and she began to speak in a breezy voice: "I am flattered, dear, but you shouldn't jump to such quick conclusions. I think almost everything you eat should be the best thing you've ever eaten," she explained. "Food is a gift, so long as nothing (or no one) was hurt in the process of it traveling to your plate."

Emily, Steven, and Tree spent a little while longer talking about the importance of food. They talked of their favorite foods, the prettiest foods, and foods they've never eaten. It was quite an exciting conversation, and Emily enjoyed it the most. Once there was nothing left of food to speak of, Steven decided to ask Tree about the odd hollowed out tree that he and Emily saw earlier. He first asked if she knew that such a tree existed. Tree's leaves trembled the moment Steven asked his question.

"How did you find it?" Tree's voice now sounded windy, which seemed to indicate that she knew more about it than Steven expected.

"Well, Emily and I were walking in the garden when we heard a group of bluebirds chirping by the hollowed out tree. I had never seen anything like that tree in Alcovia before, and it struck my curiosity."

The only thing Tree could do was shake her leaves a bit. She didn't know how to respond to such an important question, and decided to stay silent in hopes that Steven would lose his curiosity (which was terribly unlikely). Finally, she began to answer his question in the best way she believed she could.

"There is an old saying amongst us trees: *'If happiness is your destination, searching for good will take you where you long to go.'* That old, hollowed-out tree inspired that saying. You see, many years ago, when I was just a sprout, something happened to that tree," she paused for a moment, hoping to catch a breeze, and prepared for the words to follow. "It was something that could only happen to *that* particular tree. One day, an uncountable amount of years ago, there was a violent windstorm. It was the first of many to follow. A short while after the storm was over, there was a scratching sound coming from that hollow tree. It was so terribly loud, and oh, how it echoed! We all wondered what the sound was. The trees that stood next to that hollow tree say that they saw a person come out from the hollow, only to disappear minutes later." By this time, Tree's leaves shook so swiftly that many fell from their branches. "We all believe that this person was escaping something awful in search for good. Oh, if only he could have stayed in Alcovia," Tree stopped speaking. Nothing but a gentle breeze danced through her leaves and for a few moments, the mouths of Steven, Emily, and Tree seemed to be sewn shut.

"Yes, that is the story," continued Tree. "There are no known facts to be added to it."

By this time, Emily was no longer sitting in her seat, but instead standing up.

"What about the twins?" Emily asked. "What happened to them?" her tone of voice demanded an answer.

"Well, there *is* something to be said about them. You see, so many trees have observed that, for a little while after a windstorm, the hollow glows. In fact, some of their leaves have fallen into the hollow, never to be seen again. It is believed that the same thing happened to the twins."

Emily could not stop asking questions. "And what about Captain Cecil? How did he disappear?"

Tree's vague eyes wandered back and forth in thought. She was not expecting so many questions, and she was not used to speaking about such a gloomy subject.

"His situation is an odd one," she lamented. "No one knows precisely *how* he disappeared," her sentence ended abruptly; everything she needed to say suddenly ran out, which left them with nothing but silence.

In a peculiar way, the silence told Emily that there were no answers left to her questions, and upon realizing this, she sunk back into her seat and enjoyed the breeze that swirled through her black, mirror-like hair. Her mind finally calmed down, and for a while, she had no desire to speak, but only to close her eyes and soak in the peaceful air. Tree swung her branches and leaves around in the breeze, and for that moment, Emily could not think of anything she loved more than the sound of leaves swaying about.

One of Alcovia's three moons rose brightly above them, and if you happened to glance at it quickly enough, it smiled down upon them, too. This moon was particularly generous, and it never hesitated to give a bit of extra light to anyone that needed it. Somehow, this extra light struck a certain exploratory chord in Steven, who rose up from his chair. "Leaving so soon?" gasped Tree (who despised the idea of guests leaving her table). "Why, it seems like you've only just arrived!"

"Oh, Tree. If time grew on your branches instead of leaves, we would stay forever. Until then, though, Emily and I must be on our way," Steven said.

"Fair enough, my dears," she said hesitantly. "Promise me that you'll come again soon."

"Sooner than you think!" said Emily.

Tree smiled faintly, and used her branches to push them back along the path in hopes of pointing them in the direction they needed to go. When Emily and Steven were nearly out of her sight, they waved their hands and whispered goodbye.

Eight

THE PRIM PARTY

The forest continued forever, and Emily believed that she had seen at least ninety-percent of the trees in Alcovia. In a way, the trees were like a kaleidoscope, because the more she stared at them, the more she saw. This time around, she could only see leaves. A few clusters of the leaves were so tall and vast that, if she stared at them long enough, they turned into a wavy sea. In fact, they looked nearly identical to the Green Sea that she was trying to forget. Still, she could not bring herself to stop looking at them– that is, until something caught her attention. In between the sea of leaves, she could see a roof. At first, the roof looked like it was incredibly far away. A few steps ahead, though, it got bigger. It continued to grow and grow until it turned into a house. Upon seeing this, Steven did not seem the least bit interested by such a spectacle, and the expression on his face said that he had seen it many times before.

"Do you like parties, Emily?" he asked.

"Well…" Emily tried to gather her words. No one had ever invited her to a party before, and this troubled her a bit. "I don't really know. I've never been to one," she mumbled.

"What an accomplishment!" said Steven with cheer in his voice. "I've never cared for parties. They are too loud and silly. Although, the parties in Alcovia are a bit different; especially the party that Ophelia throws."

"Party?" asked Emily, finding it odd that he did not use the word 'parties' instead.

"Oh yes, she only has one type of party. Sometimes, she invites different people to it, but really, it's all quite the same."

"How is it the same?" asked Emily.

Steven replied with one indefinite answer, "You'll see."

They stood outside of the mansion for a moment, just to admire its beauty. You see, it was unlike any normal home. It stood far above the trees until you could see clouds gathered around the towers as though they were old friends. The outside of the mansion was a luminous shade of white, and everything was so clean that it almost looked odd. In addition, there were exquisite gardens with sparkling fountains, and bushes in the shape of every animal you could imagine.

Once they reached the doorway (which was tall enough for, perhaps, a giraffe to fit through), they didn't need to ring a doorbell, because the doors automatically opened for them.

The wider the doors opened, the wider Emily's eyes became. "How interesting!" she exclaimed.

The doors opened so gradually that the suspense of seeing the mansion in its entirety made it all the more beautiful. Eventually, the splendor of the mansion revealed itself in the form of glittering lights and music. If you looked around long enough, you would find that the design of the mansion was really quite peculiar. To explain, the walls twisted in a way that could only lead those who followed them in a circle. And the windows were so tall, that any normal-sized person could not see outside without the assistance of a ladder.

"This is a misshapen house, isn't it?" Emily whispered to Steven.

"Only at first glance," he said. "Now, I wonder where Ophelia could be."

Even though the party seemed to be in place, Emily and Steven were the only people there. They looked around for others until they could hear the sound of footsteps tapping. Suddenly, a woman swung open a door. She, like her gardens and mansion, was also sparkling and clean. The clothing she wore matched perfectly. The hair on her head was radiantly white and not one bit of it was out of place. And her speaking voice was almost as polished as her glossy floor. For some reason, though, she sounded abnormally anxious about something, "Who is there?" she asked with a frantic voice (which happened to be unusually low-pitched and shaky). "If you are going to be my guests," she continued, "you must be wearing your fanciest clothing, or else I'll have to -- Oh! Steven, it's you! It is so nice to see your dear face again. I couldn't tell who you were at first, because I didn't have my glasses," she said with a calmer tone of voice.

Steven could only speak to the woman through a smile, "It is nice to see you again, Ophelia. My friend Emily and I are here for your party. Are we too early?"

"Not at all dear, in fact, you are the first guests to arrive. Everyone else should be here in exactly twenty minutes. Twenty minutes on the dot, I may add," said Ophelia before focusing her attention on Emily, "It is nice to meet you, dear. I see that Steven told you to dress in your fanciest clothing, because you look lovely. I couldn't imagine what I would do if you hadn't have been dressed properly!"

Emily straightened out her skirt, "It is nice to meet you, Ophelia. And, thank you."

Ophelia, despite her impeccable wardrobe and polished voice, seemed to be a mess of emotions. The idea of perfection overtook her, and never let her mind rest.

"Please excuse me for a moment, dear lovelies. I must finish polishing the furniture. Do make yourself at home, but I beg of you not to touch any of my glass figurines!" she said while disappearing through a door.

At the exact moment she left, Emily could not help but ask

Steven why she seemed so anxious.

"It's because she held a party when she was our age," he said, "and everyone that showed up had no manners at all. They threw drinking glasses on the floor, and they painted the ceiling with cake frosting. You see, Ophelia loves to host parties, but ever since that horrible incident, she never stops fearing that all of her guests will suddenly go mad and cause a riot."

"How awful," said Emily with sympathy. "But why is she so strict about her guests wearing fancy clothing?"

"I believe it must be because she knows that anyone in their right mind wouldn't dare break glasses or paint the ceiling in their fanciest clothing, fearing that it may get torn or stained," explained Steven through a giggle. "I imagine that, if we could see Ophelia's mind, it would be nothing but sparks and smoke," he continued with a serious tone. "Worrying can do such sad and disturbing things to a mind. In fact, I would hate to see my own."

Suddenly, the doors opened again, and an earsplittingly loud "Hello!" pierced through the air.

Upon hearing this, Ophelia ran into the room to greet her next guest. "Well, if it isn't Falsetto! I am so very glad you could make it."

This guest was perhaps the most peculiar person Emily had ever seen. He had midnight-black hair, and wore a shiny, oddly shaped tuxedo (to explain: the top of the tuxedo was shaped like an upside-down triangle, and it was shiny enough to reflect the light in the room). By the way he spoke, it was obvious that he was a singer.

"Helloooooo, Oooopheeeeelia! I am ecstatic to be here. I cannot WAIT for our duet. I just know that it will be com-PLETE-ly mag-NIF-icent!" replied Falsetto.

"Yes, I am certain it will be perfect in every sense of the word. Now, if you'll excuse me for a moment, I must go do my voice exercises!" within a second, Ophelia stormed out of the room again, leaving Emily, Steven, and Falsetto together.

"Hello Falsetto," said Steven in a polite manner. "The last time we spoke, you told me about a new opera you were working on. How is that coming along?"

"How kind of you to ask! You would not believe how mag-

NIF-icent it is. In fact, Ophelia and I will be singing a duet from it at this very party."

"I'm looking forward to that!" said Emily from the corner.

"And who might this be?" Falsetto asked Steven while looking at Emily adoringly. "She has quite a darling face, does she not?"

"Ah, how silly of me. I completely forgot to introduce you both. Falsetto this is Emily. Emily, this is the one and only Falsetto," said Steven with emphasis.

"It is nice to meet you, Emily. I take it that you absolutely love, adore and admire opera?"

"Well, I guess so. I really don't know much about it, to be honest."

Falsetto's eyes widened and he began to speak with a terribly loud tone of voice, "How can you allow yourself not to know absolutely everything about the fantastical art that is opera? Oh, dear Emily, you have much to learn— so very much to learn indeed!"

"Well, Falsetto," said Steven, "Emily hasn't quite had the chance to get to know it. Perhaps you can teach her a few things?"

"All in due time, all in due time," replied Falsetto.

As the minutes passed, a crowd of people filled up the mansion. And each one received a clothing inspection from Ophelia. She had to turn one man away because his socks did not match, and the sleeve of his suit jacket had a small tear. Other than that, Ophelia found the rest of her guests impeccable and allowed them to stay. When the guests spoke, the mansion became flooded with different conversations, and Emily could not help but eavesdrop on a few of them. Some people were saying that it was horribly unfair of Ophelia to turn the poor man away just because of a few imperfections in his outfit. Others raved about how lovely her home was. Still some complained that it was all too clean, saying that a bit of mess adds character to a home. Emily agreed with all she heard, and from that moment on, she found the act of eavesdropping to be just as fascinating as spying on people.

"How does Ophelia know so many people?" whispered Emily to Steven.

Steven giggled at what he was about to say, "She hardly knows them, actually. Usually, she just invites the most well-dressed people she meets in Alcovia. Believe me: Alcovia is full of well-dressed citizens."

Now, if you stood in the middle of the crowds long enough, you would begin to feel as though you were bobbling along in the middle of a wavy, sparkling sea. This bobbling feeling lasted for a few moments until Ophelia announced that an opera would be taking place in her party room. Finally, everyone was silent, and the sea of sound was calm.

"How do we get to the party room?" asked Emily.

"Oh, we just stand here…and wait," replied Steven.

"Wait for what?"

"To be transported to the party room, of course!" yelled one of the guests who, like Emily, loved to eavesdrop.

Suddenly, the floor below them elevated so high until they could almost touch the ceiling. Once the elevation stopped, all of the guests walked forward into a darkened room.

In this room, all of the walls were painted black, and all of the statues were on tables so high that no one could reach them. A circular stage sat in the middle of the room, and it spun around slowly. The guests tried their best to walk sluggishly, so as not to knock the tables down or get glitter from their clothing on the freshly cleaned walls.

"So, what do you think?" Steven asked Emily

"I've never seen a room that was painted black before," replied Emily, who was rather fond of the idea of it.

"Yes, something about darkness wakes up the imagination like nothing else. For this reason, I always look forward to rainy days," said Steven. "Although, I am almost certain that Ophelia painted this room black so that smudges and scratches wouldn't show up."

Once all of the guests crowded together in the room, soft pink lights flickered on and off, and before they knew it, music began to play. The sound of the music filled the air, but for some odd reason the actual orchestra was nowhere to be found.

"Where is the orchestra, Steven?" asked Emily.

"No one knows for sure," he said, looking up to the ceiling, and down at the floor, and up to the ceiling again. "Some think that they play in a hidden chamber. Others have said that their tune was recorded many years ago, and is played over speakers. I like to think that they are hidden somewhere in this room. Wouldn't that be interesting? I wonder how they would go about hiding…"

The tune stirred around the room like a thunderstorm, and suddenly Falsetto and Ophelia appeared on the ever-spinning stage. What a spectacle they were! Ophelia was barely recognizable, because her dress was so big. And Falsetto looked as though he plucked stars from the sky and sewed them onto his suit. As soon as the both of them stood in the center of the stage, Falsetto drew in a breath.

"It has been said that some of the BEST things have no name," said Falsetto, half-singing. "The song that Ophelia and I will sing to you has no name. Still, it truly is WON-der-FUL!"

Bursts of violin filled the air, and a sparkling harp soon joined it. They played together softly, then loudly, then softly again. Up and down went the tune, until its sound broke into pieces by the voices of Falsetto and Ophelia, who belted out a song with words that went something like this:

"Little cloud, float my way
Please, oh please, oh please.
Violet skies, light my eyes
Please, oh please, oh please.
Off we go to daydream
Until suddenly we see
All that we have ever dreamt
Has suddenly come to be!

Alcovia is the place for me,
Alcovia is the place for me.

Off to Alcovia, you and I
Where we will sail
And where we will fly.
Cozy clouds, wavy sea.
It is wonderful for you
It is wonderful for me.

We sing the song
The wind, wind, windy song
And as we sing we sway
Through the sky that's never night
Through the sky that's never day.

Ah! What a place to be
There is nothing more extraordinary.
It's the place for you
It's the place for me.

Now, take my hand
And we will wander.
There is nowhere else I'd go
Than to Alcovia with you, with you
Than to Alcovia with you.
And as we wander, we shall know
That all of our dreams are true."

By this time, the words must have stirred within the guests an emotion that could only cause them to dance around rather clumsily. In fact, they twirled about so much that they aimlessly ran into the tables that Ophelia's glass figurines stood on top of, causing them to fall and break into a million bits. As soon as Ophelia caught sight of this, she hastily stopped singing.

"ENOUGH!" she yelled loudly as Falsetto carried on. "Please, everyone! Stop dancing!"

They didn't hear her, though, and proceeded to step on the

pieces of broken glass, stirring up the mess even more.

The party room that was spotless a moment ago was now a disaster that had no hope of being clean anytime soon. You couldn't even walk without crunching up broken glass, or tripping over chairs.

With each movement the guests made, Ophelia found herself dizzier and dizzier because she had no way of controlling them. To make matters worse, Falsetto was so deeply buried in the music that he kept on singing as though nothing was happening. His singing did nothing but fuel the dancing, which in turn, caused more messes.

"Are you QUITE finished?" cried Ophelia to her operatic friend.

The piercing of Ophelia's angry voice finally broke through Falsetto's and all sound vanished, leaving only silence and messes (which is a terribly frightful mix).

"How can you treat someone's home with such disrespect?" said Ophelia sternly. "In a way, you have disrespected me! Therefore, I demand all who had a part in this mess to clean it up, even if it takes hours - or days!"

Emily and Steven were fine examples of partygoers, though. They had no part in the dancing or mess-making. And Ophelia, in noticing their tidiness, allowed them to leave early without having to clean up any messes.

"It was still a lovely party," said Steven. "A bit of mess didn't ruin it too badly. And your voice sounded wonderful."

Ophelia's stern expression softened. "Thank you, my dear. I wish I knew more people like you and Emily."

Steven glanced at the cuff of his jacket, and made a wondering face. "I feel as though I must confess something to you, Ophelia," he said.

"And what is that?"

Steven glanced at his cuff once again. On the edge, there was a small pink stain from strawberry ice cream, and it was obvious that it had been there for months.

"My outfit isn't entirely perfect, you see," he whispered, holding up his wrist to Ophelia's eye level. "I've had this stain for a very long time. I got it by accident, but it doesn't mean I'm an untidy person."

"I...I don't know what to say," said Ophelia, staring at the pink smudge through her glasses. She examined it for a few moments, and as she examined it, she thought. Her mind clicked like gears in a clock until she realized something. "How wrong it was of me to turn that poor man away!" she cried. "All he had was a small tear on his suit, and mismatched socks. Why, he could have been the tidiest guest at the party! And to think that he didn't even put up a fight when I turned him away, the poor dear. Thank you, Steven. Next time I have a party, I will only invite kind people instead of remarkably dressed strangers. Until then, I'm going to track that poor man down and invite him for tea."

"Good idea!" said Steven. "I'm sure he will enjoy that."

Ophelia smiled at Emily and Steven lovingly. "Both of you are so precious, and you make such good use of your manners. I have learned so much from you, and I'm glad to know you. Now, you had better get going, or else I may feel tempted to make you clean with the rest of the party!" she laughed.

Before Emily and Steven could walk past Ophelia's gardens, Falsetto quickly came running towards them as though he had something important to announce. "Steven! Emily! Stop!" he shrieked.

"What is it, Falsetto?" said Emily.

"I wanted to tell you that my opera is FINISSSSHED! The first showing will be at my opera house. Do make a point to show up, won't you? And you do know that I am expecting you to bring a perfectly flawless opera cake, Steven!" he spoke so forcefully, and Emily wondered if the tone of his voice ever gave him a sore throat at the end of the day.

"I will make you one before the opera," replied Steven.

"How marvelous! I shall await it with immeasurable excitement. I just know the opera is going to be fantastical. You *WON'T* be disappointed. *BRRAVOOO!*" at that, Falsetto gracefully ran back into Ophelia's mansion.

"Do you think he will invite everyone from the party?" Emily asked Steven.

"I'm certain of it, and I hope he's ready to clean up another mess!" he laughed.

Emily took one last look at Ophelia's garden, and felt happy. "I am so glad you brought me here. It's so different from the world we know, and yet, in some ways, it's so similar," she said.

"I'm glad to hear you say that, Emily. I guess it all depends on how you view things in the world we know. Everything could be this interesting, but only if your viewpoint is correct. I believe that Alcovia is just what you need. Now, let's get going, because we still have so much to see!"

Nine

THE STUNNING SEA

"You know, it is a shame," said Steven while skipping over a pile of leaves.

"What's a shame?" asked Emily.

"That you can no longer say you've never been to a party. It was such a lovely thing to be able to tell people. I would be so proud to say it."

"Why? Isn't it boring to never go to parties?"

Steven stopped to gather his words. "Not at all!" he cried, sounding very sure of himself. "When you think about it, most parties are incredibly ordinary. Why would you want to do something that was ordinary?"

Emily suddenly felt proud of herself. All her life, everything ordinary surrounded her; ordinary houses, ordinary people, ordinary jobs. Now, though, she looked back and realized that her entire life, she was a butterfly in a crowd of moths. She was different, and different is good.

After walking for a little while, they found themselves standing atop a grassy cliff that overlooked a sea.

"Listen to those waves, Emily!" cried Steven. "They are singing to us! Aren't their voices delightful?"

As the both of them looked down, they could not help but contemplate the glassy waves. They flowed about flawlessly, each with its own unique way of swishing and swirling. Suddenly, the memory of the Green Sea filled Emily's mind, and instead of feeling troubled, she was happy. "I have come to a conclusion," she said.

"And what is that?" asked Steven.

"In the dull town by the Green Sea, I was only focused on how sad the town made me. The sea never made me sad. In fact, it was really quite beautiful. I am happy now, because I realize that parts of my past were good after all."

Steven smiled and Emily smiled back, as good friends do when they know that the other is happy.

"I knew Alcovia would change your way of thinking a bit, Emily," he said with kindness in his voice. "Now, let's walk by the shore and gaze at the water up close."

Emily looked straight down, and the height made her dizzy. "How could we ever get down?" she asked.

Without any words, Steven took the whistle from around his neck and used it to call a cloud. The sound of the whistle was jangly, and it echoed for miles. Soon after the echo, a wispy cloud came swooping down to their level. "Cloud, can you please take us to the shore?" asked Steven, to which the cloud replied in a happy twirl.

"Come on, Emily!" he said while stepping onto the cloud as if the act was nothing unusual. Emily, on the other hand, took a large step back. The very thought of stepping foot on an airy little cloud struck fear in her, and her mind would not stop racing with frightening thoughts. What if she fell right through it? What if she lost her balance and tumbled down? Worse yet, what if it mistakenly dropped her in the middle of the sea? Upon seeing Emily's nervous expression, Steven spoke reassuringly to her. "It's okay, Emily. You won't fall. I promise," he whispered while petting the cloud with his foot. "I've ridden this cloud hundreds of times before. It's impossible to fall off of it. Even if you did slip, it would catch you before you fell to the ground. It is incredibly prompt about such things."

Since there was no other way to get down, Emily decided that she would rather ride on a cloud than be stuck on the cliff forever, so she trusted in Steven once again and took a step onto the cloud. At first, her foot sunk in, which startled her a bit, but after a moment she was steady. Once the cloud could tell she stood steadily, it cuddled up to her in the same way a soft white puppy would.

"See, it isn't too scary, is it?" Steven said. "Between the cloud and I, you have barely any chance of falling."

They slowly floated closer and closer to the shore, and as they floated, it blissfully danced along with the breeze. What a joy it is to ride on a cloud (once you're used to it, of course)!

As soon as they reached the seashore, the cloud let Emily and Steven step off before it disappeared altogether.

"I will never view a cloud the same way again!" exclaimed Emily, amazed at what had just taken place.

"I'm happy to hear you say that, Emily! When you think of it, clouds are wonderful. I am always amazed that something as simple as water can turn into something as fantastic as a cloud. As for the sea, what do you think? Aren't the waves even lovelier up close?"

The empty seaside was luminous, and the sand wore seashells like jewelry. The water around them was calm, and the light from the moon made it look like it was full of diamonds. All of the beauty overtook Emily, which suddenly inspired her to respond to Steven in a new way:

"I used to live by a sea
But it was of no joy to me!
Each day I would sit and stare
At the sea's blinding glare.
But now as I look to this sea today

My mind has changed in every way!
No longer is it dull and green—
It is a place that's most serene.
And each feature that it shows to me
Is full of charm and glory.
What a joyful place to be!
Here at this sea.
What a lovely place to be!
Here at this sea."

Steven applauded loudly. "What lovely words! I knew that you could come up with such nice thoughts. All you needed was a bit of inspiration."

"Thank you, Steven. I never knew how inspiring a sea could be. Let's stare at it a little longer."

There were so many different things to look for in the sea. Steven told Emily of how he once found a box full of mirrors. Inside, there were small mirrors, golden mirrors, and pieces of mirrors.

"I don't know who it belonged to," he said, "so I buried it in the sand to make sure it wouldn't get lost again."

The longer they stared at the sea, the more they saw. Emily found a seashell necklace, and Steven (to his disappointment) found an old boot. They stared and stared and stared until suddenly, a cluster of flickering lights appeared in the distance. "What could it be?" asked Emily. "Do you think it's a ship?"

Steven's eyes widened with excitement. "I believe it is a ship," he cried. "I wonder who's sailing it. Oh, let's watch it get closer! I do love to watch ships sail."

The orange flickering lights grew bigger as the ship got closer, and from the sandy shore, they saw someone on the ship throw a large gray anchor next to a rickety old dock. As soon as the anchor landed, a man climbed down the side and onto land, catching sight of Emily and Steven as he did so.

"Who is he?" Emily whispered.

"From the look of it, I would say that he is more than likely a sailor. Oh, and it looks like he is coming our way to say hello!"

The sailor took off his red knit hat and raked his fingers through his dark, cherry-kissed hair. "Well! Yours are the first faces I have seen in weeks! Or could it be months? Ah, I've lost track."

Both Emily and Steven stared at the sailor the same way they stared at his ship: still and silently so they would not miss a movement.

"Aye, you two look terrified!" the sailor said, laughing through his unusually white teeth. "You must forgive me; I always look a bit rumpled after a long voyage. Now, if you don't mind me asking, what might your names be?"

Steven introduced himself first, trying to make a lasting impression on the sailor. You see, from all of his trips to Alcovia, he had always heard stories of sailors. And out of all his trips to Alcovia, he had only seen them from the shore, gliding over the waves in their magnificent ships. The adventurous life of sailors is what captivated him the most because their sense of adventure easily related to his own.

"...and I must add that I really do dislike the name Steven," he said with a faint tremble of excitement in his voice. The sailor listened to him with a supportive smile. "I don't know why anyone thought I would make a good Steven. I don't think that name describes an adventurer like me."

"Ah, but that's where you're wrong!" cried the sailor with determination in attempt to change Steven's mind. "Our names don't describe us. Instead, our actions do. Our actions can mold us into either a flower vase or a garbage pail. Never blame your name, dear boy." Steven let those words sink into his mind for a moment as the sailor turned his attention to Emily. "And what is your name?" he asked softly while shifting his head sideways in question.

"Emily," she sprinted. She had nothing else to add, for she neither liked nor disliked her name.

"It's a pleasure to know you, Emily and Steven. Now, let me introduce myself to you. My name is Silas."

After the name 'Silas' was said aloud, time stopped. Memories of the museum consumed the minds of Steven and Emily, and they could not believe whom they were speaking to.

"You're Silas?" cried Steven, sounding unusually loud against the sleepy sea.

"Aye, and if you switch the letters around, it spells 'sails'," he laughed.

"Are you the same Silas who—"

"Indeed."

"Your father is Captain Cecil?"

"Ah yes, my father is indeed the missing Captain Cecil." Silas looked out to the sea wonderingly. "Methinks I've been sailing for too long and spending too much of my life searching for that world of darkness and harsh waves. I know it exists, and not even a windstorm will keep me from finding it. Mark my words." Even though the conversation was gloomy, Silas kept a cool, kind expression on his face. "Still," he continued, "the sea has a way of reminding you that anything is possible. If it were not for the sea, I would have given up long ago. We can defy the current, only if our mind is set on doing so."

Steven nodded in agreement. "Do you believe that the world of darkness is where your father went?" he asked.

Silas drew in a breath. "The sea is the keeper of many secrets and hiding places, Steven. Ah, and it is a very good keeper at that. One day, I will be able to answer your question, but for now, I am at loss for words."

The soft mist in the air soon turned into a downpour of rain, and Silas motioned Emily and Steven to follow him. He walked dizzily, as though he was dodging hundreds of imaginary boulders, and this caused Emily to giggle under her breath every time he would take a particularly large step. "We are just going to this lighthouse yonder way!" yelled Silas through the raindrops. The lighthouse he pointed to was tall, and its light beamed through the fog like a shiny golden rod. By the time they made it, their clothes were drenched. Silas, who was used to such occurrences, took off his red hat and wrung out the extra water. "The sky is a'sobbing! Ah, it does bring me joy to be back in the old lighthouse again." Silas looked at the inside of the lighthouse happily and breathed in its wood scented air. "This lighthouse watched me grow up. If it could speak, I hope that it would have at least one good thing to say about me," he laughed. "Something very special resides at the top, and I would like you meet it!" As he spoke, he stretched out his hand towards an endless spiral staircase. It was so tall that Emily and Steven could only gaze at it with wide, amazed eyes.

"How long would it take us to get to the top?" asked Emily.

Silas silently counted the first few steps. "Oh, it wouldn't take more than a few moments. You know, it would be such a shame if you never got to see what lies at the peak."

Steven mused at the staircase, shaking his head in reflection. "As an adventurer, it would be quite important for me to explore this lighthouse. After all, I would imagine it would provide some interesting information for my notebooks."

The pouring rain beat on the side of the lighthouse, sounding heavier than ever. "I am terribly curious to see, and I'd hate to go outside when it's raining," said Emily.

"Then after you!" cheered Silas. "I must warn you that the first step is a bit creaky."

The staircase seemed never-ending, and from where they stood, it looked like it could take you all the way up into the sky. Up a few steps, they found a collection of interesting things. Against the curved, wooden wall stood a tall shelf that held a collection of glass bottles containing nothing but seashells.

Emily whispered to herself in remembrance, "Captain Cecil collected seashells."

"Aye," replied Silas. "Most of his seashells are on this shelf; well, the most important seashells at least. Here, let me show you a few that I find to be the most alluring." Silas wiped his hands on his wrinkled navy jacket and proceeded to grab from the top shelf a dusty, dark jar. "These shells are the rarest of them all. They do not exist in Alcovia, but only in that world of darkness. These are proof that such a world exists. Would you just look at them? They are like pieces of the night chipped away from the sky."

Emily and Steven looked at each other rapidly. They were both thinking the same thing: Pepper's theory was right. Steven studied the jar of black seashells intently as he thought of what to say next. "And Captain Cecil never spoke of this world of darkness?" he asked.

"Never!" proclaimed Silas. "But I know it exists. When your father leaves for a long while, and comes back with things you've never seen or heard of before, such as black seashells, it is only proper to conclude that he has been to another place, another world."

Emily looked up to Silas and smiled, for the sadness in his voice troubled her. "You'll find him, Silas. I just know that you will," she said simply, hoping that it would cheer him up.

"Thank you, Emily. Your kindness alone could sail a thousand ships. Now, what are we waiting for? Let's continue."

They ventured up each step. Sometimes they would walk quickly, and if they were passing something interesting, they would walk slowly. At one point, they found themselves greeted by an array of old, wrinkled portraits of sailors and their beloved ships. "Who are they?" Emily asked.

"They are relatives," replied Silas, "although, I can't say I know very much about them."

One portrait in particular caught Emily's attention: a black and white photo of three men with a label underneath that read:

CAPT. CECIL, FIRST MATE, AND FRIEND

"There is Captain Cecil!" said Emily, pointing to a tall man with windswept hair and a smiling face. It was not difficult to pick him out, because he was the only man who stood proudly with a handful of seashells. "What became of the first mate and friend?"

"Ah, your questions are full of wonder, Emily," said Silas.

He first pointed to a young man with dark hair and a solemn face. His arms were tightly crossed, and his chin nearly touched his neck. "That is the man who used to be my father's first mate. He was not a kind man, and speaking to him was like speaking to a windstorm. He huffed at any word you said if, of course, he was listening to you to begin with. My last memory of him is blurry, but I do remember him leaving this very lighthouse in an angry fit, never to be seen again. I must admit that he was interesting to observe, but everything that made him interesting caused him to be a terrible first mate."

The third man in the photo, labeled simply as 'friend', had hair that looked translucent against the white sky. You couldn't really see his face, but you could see that he was dressed differently compared to Captain Cecil and the first mate. In addition, he held on tightly to a small black notebook in his right hand. "This man," continued Silas while pointing at the pale figure, "was a friend of my father's. He was a devoted adventurer. Ah, just like you are, Steven! His adventures took place on both land and sea." Silas hesitated for a moment. "You…you see, he was with my father on that wretched day."

"That's the man who went missing along with your father," sighed Steven. "How saddening."

"Aye. Oh, if only I could remember that kind man's name."

"How did he and your father know each other?" asked Emily.

"Well, if my memory serves me correctly, their paths crossed because they were both adventurous men. I believe they met at the cave in the middle of the sea. Oh, that reminds me! I'd like to take you both there, if the rain lets up of course. Now, as interesting as these photographs are, we must keep climbing! There are only a few more steps!" Upon noticing Emily and Steven's wariness, Silas cleared his throat and sang a song:

"Oh, when I was a lad of only three
My father took my wee brother and me
On a tour of the starry sea,
On a tour of the starry sea.

When we sail'd back onto land
I kissed that gold, sugary sand
And promised that I'd never stand
On the deck of a ship again,
On the deck of a ship again.

'The waves are too big!' I'd cry.

'I want to stay where it's warm and dry!'

I never gave the sea a try,

Until something changed my mind,

Until something changed my mind.

One day I walked by the seaside

Against the edge of that watery tide

Even if I tried, I could not hide

Away from the sea's call,

Away from the sea's call.

Mindless, I ran into those waves

And found treasures, and shells, and caves.

Now, I am not afraid

To sail amongst the sea,

To sail amongst the sea."

Immediately after finishing the song, Silas counted aloud the last few steps to the top. "Three, two, one! Ah, what a joy it is to climb to the top of this lighthouse." Against the top step, a shimmering golden door greeted them. The handle had many scratches, and above it was an untidily written sign that said, *"Please open door softly, as its squeak can be startling."* Without any hesitation at all, Silas got a tight hold of the door handle, and opened it in a gentle yet swift way. As soon as he did this, music began to play.

Ten

THE MUSIC BOX ROOM

Few things are better than a great song. A great song is, perhaps, just as vital as sunlight and rain. Sometimes the tune empowers us, and the words speak to us in a way that nothing (or no one) else can. The song that played in the top of the lighthouse was quite possibly the most pleasant tune you'd ever have the pleasure of hearing. Each jingle stirred up a warm, sugary feeling that was impossible to ignore.

"Emily, Steven, I'd like you to meet the music box room," cheered Silas. His face glimmered with stored memories of his life in that lovely room and he gazed at it as though he was gazing at a beloved family member. Along the walls, there were hundreds (if not thousands) of golden mechanical gears that turned continuously in order to generate the music. Like a magnet, Steven walked over to the ever-spinning wall, and studied each gear intently. "How," (he tried to think of a suitable word for such a magnificent piece of art). "Majestic! How completely majestic." His excitement was nearly uncontainable.

Emily also stared at the gears as they spun around. "I've seen tiny music boxes once or twice," she commented, "but I've never seen a music box room!"

"That's because there's only one! There is only one music box room ever to exist!" shouted Silas while fluttering his hands all around.

It was quite fantastic how such a small room held so many interesting things to look at. Once you stopped gazing at the golden gears in the wall, you would find four chairs, three violins, two accordions, and a dark dusty corner that led into a dark dusty room. The ceiling was made out of fine blue stained glass, and encased in the glass was a bright light that, like the gears in the walls, turned continuously.

"Now!" said Silas. "If only I could find–" suddenly, in the middle of his sentence, a tall young fellow came bashfully creeping from the darkened room. "Elliott! Why must you always hide and cause me to worry about you?"

The fellow was silent. His ocean blue eyes gazed at Emily and Steven, two perfect strangers, and he could not bring himself to say a word.

"Emily, Steven, I'd like for you both to meet my wee brother Elliott. He is a talented musician who has rhymed his sentences ever since he could speak," explained Silas. "I do feel quite bad for him. Could you just imagine not being able to speak normally?" he added in a whisper.

Suddenly, Elliott drew in a nervous breath. "How fine it is to greet someone you'd love to meet. I rhyme my words this way, because it keeps sad thoughts at bay." What a charming voice Elliott had! He did not stumble in his rhymes, and it sounded like he spent days planning his sentences so they would make sense. "Thank you for being my guests," he continued. "Are there any songs you request?"

"Hello, Elliott. How fine it is to meet you," Emily said softly. "I think we would all enjoy hearing your favorite song," she added, knowing that he would most likely put more feeling into the song that was dearest to his heart.

Elliott's face beamed with happiness. Whenever he thought of his favorite song, his heart fluttered and danced. For most of his life, music had been his most faithful companion. It was there for him to play on bright sunny days, and it was there for him to listen to on dark stormy nights. Elliott's best friend was music, and music's best friend was Elliott. He could not imagine life without it, and he was nearly convinced that tunes, and chords, and harmonies flowed through his very veins. "Well, that is what I will play! It is perfect for this rainy day. Now please go on and take a seat before you enjoy this song so sweet." As soon as the three of them sat down, he strapped the accordion around his shoulder and braced himself for the tune he was about to play. He first cracked his fingers, and then combed his dark curly hair. Then, he polished the keys of the accordion (and spent quite some time doing so).

"Is something wrong, brother?" asked Silas, halfway standing up from his seat.

"I'm making sure my mind is in place to play a song that is

124

so full of grace," replied Elliott. This was the first time he would ever play this song for an audience, and he wanted to prepare himself so that it would sound impeccable. Suddenly, he pressed down on the lowest key of the accordion, and from there, the tune went up and down. The song he played had no words, yet it sounded as though it was speaking to you. When Elliott played the high-pitched tune, the room was bright. When he played the low-pitched tune, the room got a little darker. And when he played the in-between sounds, it caused a fantastically bittersweet feeling. As Elliott rocked his accordion back and forth, he had the happiest look upon his face. The song would have been very different if he had been playing it with an unhappy frown, or a scrunched-up scowl. He played and played until the song was finished. The ending of the song saddened Emily and Steven, who could have easily listened to it for hours while enjoying every second.

Silas was the first to applaud once the song was over. "Now, wasn't I right? Isn't he a talented musician?" he asked (sounding terribly proud of his brother).

Emily and Steven joined in the applause. "You play that accordion beautifully, Elliott!" Emily said while Steven nodded his head in agreement.

After hearing such kind words, Elliott's cheeks turned bright red, and his smile became unbreakable. "You three are too kind. Now, if you don't mind, I'm going to fix a cup of tea. Would you care to enjoy a cup with me?"

"Oh Elliott, you've always been fond of tea," said Silas. "Emily, Steven, you must try Elliott's tea! You must take a sip, even if it isn't your favorite thing to drink."

"There are few things I love more than tea," cried Steven.

"I would love to try a cup," added Emily.

"Well, alright! We'll all have a cup of tea with you, Elliott!" yelled Silas cheerfully.

At that, Elliott disappeared again into that dark dusty corner.

"What is inside that dark old room?" whispered Steven with his eyes glued to that shadowy doorway.

"Believe it or not, I have not been in that room for many ages. In fact, its memory has nearly escaped my mind once or twice. That's the bad thing about memories. They always want to fade away. I wonder where memories go once they've faded away."

"Why don't you go in the room now?" asked Steven.

"Ah, I could never do that. That is Elliott's room. It would be best if I let it be."

"Do you have any memories of the room? Any memories at all?" inquired Emily, to which Silas smiled.

"I seem to remember a big hole in the middle of the floor, and sometimes it would— oh, never mind. Memories always blur the past. Whether they are good memories or bad, the result is always the same. Memories cannot be trusted."

In what seemed to be no time at all, Elliott came walking out with a golden tray that held four small teacups.

"Elliott, you've always known how to make a swift cup of tea. Aye, it reminds me of that story from when we were children. Do you remember it?"

Elliott took a sip of tea and smiled. "That story is so dear to my heart; to me it is a work of art. For this moment it is so fit, would you like me to recite it?"

"By all means recite it, dear brother! I'm sure Emily and Steven will enjoy it as well," replied Silas with enthusiasm that caused his voice to echo throughout the room.

So, they silently listened to Elliott as he recited his cherished tale:

"There once lived a little boy
Who always moved so fast.
Within the world, he found no joy
Because his speed was vast.
He took no time to smell a rose
Or stare at the sky above.
He only cared about the rate he could go—
His speediness was his love.

As the boy turned into a man,
He began to slow down a bit
But not enough to wreck the span
At which he could pace and sprint.
He never enjoyed life's little gifts
And the happiness they bring.
He only enjoyed moving so swift

And being full of zing.

As many years passed, the man became old
And could barely move at all.
Each day he would slowly stroll
But if he went too fast, he'd fall.

So upon feeling so sad and blue
He looked up to the sky,
And saw its art and lovely hue,
And for a moment, he cried.

He now realized all he had missed
While he was living so fast,
And all that he could have seen
Before his youth had passed."

Elliott's eyes glistened with tears, but he did not rush to wipe them away. Instead, he let them roll down his cheeks until they splashed silently onto the floor.

"Elliott! You are going to cause my eyes to well up and cry!" said Silas, whose voice sounded terribly distorted (as most voices do when they are trying not to cry). "I am sorry for our tearful ways, Emily and Steven. We are so sentimental, because our father told this story to us as young children."

After Silas said this, Elliott sighed loudly. "Our conversation has become quite sad," he said. "Can we speak of things that will make us glad?"

"Aye," said Silas. "What shall we talk about, Elliott?"

Elliott did not answer, but instead began to play a whispery tune with his violin. Whenever he had to answer such important questions, he made sure to first play a bit of music in order to clear his mind. "Let's talk about the gears on the wall," he said finally, with a glow of excitement. "The song they play is beautiful to all. If I press that button over there, it will give the song a jolly flair!"

"Well, what's stopping you then?" exclaimed Silas. "Do go press the button!"

Elliot sprung up from his seat and pressed the little candy-red button on the wall. It was quite an inviting little button, and it was a wonder that it hadn't been pressed sooner. Immediately after pressing it, there was no movement. Then, like a burst of fireworks, the gears turned quicker and quicker until something quite strange happened. The song (that was once rather slow) played faster and faster, causing the entire music box room to spin around in circles.

"Elliott! Is the room meant to spin around this way?" cried Emily, holding on to her seat with all of her strength.

"Oh Emily, please don't be distraught; could you imagine how bored we'd be if it did not?"

With each spin, the room got bigger and bigger (which was no surprise to Emily, who was beginning to get used to such odd proportions).

"What's happening now?" asked Steven, whose cheeks were red with exhilaration.

"The walls are growing!" announced Silas. "They are growing beyond belief!"

By this time, the spinning room slowed down, and once everything stopped moving, there were three new doorways. "Where in the world did THOSE come from?" asked Steven, peering at each doorway with curiosity.

"Not all questions have an answer, and the finest surprises

appear without explanation," said Silas.

"I wonder what's inside those rooms," whispered Emily to herself.

Elliott overheard Emily, and could not help but respond to her. "Ah, wondering is such a chore. Why don't you pick out a door?" he whispered.

So, that is exactly what Emily did. Out of the three doors, one door was slightly wider than the rest. She concluded that this room most likely held something a bit grander than the others, and decided upon this one. "What a wonderful choice," shouted Silas, "a wonderful choice indeed." He then proceeded to open the door slowly and the four of them crept inside.

Eleven

THE TELESCOPE ROOM

What a sight! What a marvelous collection! Telescopes filled the room to the brim. There were small ones, large ones, colorful ones, and clear ones (amongst many others, of course). Some of them sat on stands that overlooked the ocean, and some of them looked up to the sky. Telescopes, telescopes, everywhere you looked, there was a telescope. Now, with so many in one room, it was reasonable to conclude that no two were the same. Each of them must have been different in their own way, and there was only one way to find out. "Why are you two just standing there?" exclaimed Silas to Emily and

Steven, who stood motionless in awe. "Go test them out, and see what you find!"

Against the window, a silver telescope splotched with bright paint caught Steven's eye and he could not help but gravitate to it. When he looked through the lens, he was shocked (perhaps, nearly, to death) at what he saw. The entire ocean turned into a moving painting with golden sands, silver waves, and pink skies. "Where did you find this telescope? Who did it belong to?" cried Steven to Silas. By this time, he found himself looking away from the lens, looking outside the window, and looking into the lens again. He repeated this act at least seven times before Silas answered him.

"Ah, can't believe what you see? I am not the least bit sure of whom it belonged to. All I know is that I found it floating all alone by the sea cave, and I didn't have the heart to ignore it."

Steven peered through the lens for a few minutes more, feeling as though there was nothing else around him. He looked as far as the eye could see, and eventually, he found the sea cave. It was painted black with splatters of silver. Near the edge of the sea cave, he spotted the tail of what appeared to be a great goldfish (which, in fact, looked big enough to be the goldfish that they learned about in the museum). "There it is!"

he shouted with delight over his discovery.

"There what is?" asked Emily. (Silas and Elliott also wondered what Steven discovered, but Emily beat them to the question.)

"The goldfish!" he said. "I am looking at it right now. I can even see its tail splashing about in the water!"

By this time, Emily, Silas, and Elliott were crowded around the paint-splattered telescope, waiting to get their turn to peer through its lens. "I can't believe that goldfish has stayed in that sea cave for so long!" said Silas. "It must be a very comfortable place to live— for a goldfish, of course."

"Have you ever met the goldfish before?" asked Emily, trying not to laugh at how silly her question sounded when she said it aloud.

"I have only said hello to her, and she, in turn, waved her fin to me."

Steven finally looked away from the lens for a moment. "Silas, do you think we can meet her after the rain stops?" he asked.

"I don't see why not. Now, let's see what else we can find."

All of the telescopes overwhelmed Emily, who had a difficult time choosing which one she should look through. Eventually she chose a blue one, but when she pointed the lens to the ocean, everything was terribly blurry. When she pointed the lens inside the room, though, everything became as clear as glass. "I think this telescope is broken!" she shouted.

"It's because it was made just for me. My mind is rather broken, you see," Elliott snickered.

"Ah, but it is beautifully broken, dear brother!"

Emily and Steven stood in confusion. Whatever Silas and Elliott were speaking about sounded intriguing, and they wanted to know more. Upon seeing their confusion, Silas began to explain the purpose of the telescope room. "You see, our telescope room was made to represent the unique way that every person sees the world around them. Elliott is not fond of going outside; therefore, looking to the sea through his telescope is very strange and blurry," Silas then pointed to a tan telescope decorated with ink drawings. "This is my telescope," he said proudly. "Why don't you look into it and tell me what you see?"

Emily and Steven each took a turn looking into the telescope, and what they both saw was nothing short of astounding. What was once a moving sea was now an intricately drawn map with all kinds of different arrows and lines.

"Is that really how you see the world, Silas?" asked Steven.

"There is no other way for me to see it. That is one thing I know for certain."

"Who do the other telescopes belong to?"

"Well, one of them belongs to my father, and another belongs to his former first mate that I told you about before. Most of them, though, have unknown owners."

"May I see the two you just mentioned?" asked Steven.

"Of course you may." Silas then led Steven to the largest telescope in the room. It was porcelain with a ring of shells encrusted around the rim.

It was, quite easily, the tallest telescope that Steven had ever seen. And if you wanted to reach the lens, you had to step on a ladder. A sense of relief overcame Steven once he had climbed the ladder, and his little blue eye reached Captain Cecil's telescope (frankly, he also felt rather proud of himself for accomplishing such a feat without falling or breaking something).

Cecil's telescope treated Steven's eyes to a lightshow. In the sea, you would find that the seashells glowed like stars. No matter how far, or how deep into the sea you gazed, there was always a cluster of glowing seashells sitting pretty in their sandy homes. "Emily!" cried Steven excitedly (after all, who would not feel excited over a glowing sea?). "You must look through Captain Cecil's telescope!"

"Just a moment, Steven!" said Emily from the other side of the room. She was quite preoccupied with a lovely telescope that turned everything into a colorful kaleidoscopic image.

Steven waited patiently, that is, until he saw a flash of light through Cecil's telescope. Once again, he looked away from the lens, and outside the window, and into the lens again (five times in a row, to be exact). "Is it storming? Did I just see lightning?" he asked.

"No, not in the slightest," said Silas. "Sometimes it gives off wee flashes of light. I wish I knew why."

Upon hearing the commotion, Emily scurried away from the kaleidoscope telescope and waited for Steven to explain the flashes of light. (I do apologize if, by now, you are quite tired of reading words that end in "scope," but there is simply no other way to tell the story. I considered calling them "long magnifying devices" but that would make it all the more perplexing, wouldn't you agree?)

Steven's eye may as well been attached to that device, because no matter how many times Emily asked for a turn to look through the lens, he did not move, almost as though he didn't hear her at all. "It just keeps flashing," he said slowly. "Flashing, and flashing, and flashing."

"What keeps flashing?" asked Emily.

"Different parts of the sea. Oh, I wish I knew why they kept on flashing!"

"May I have a look?"

Steven kept on gazing. "In just one second."

Emily found it ridiculous to keep waiting for her turn while there were so many new and exciting telescopes to look at, so she strolled around the room until she found one that looked most interesting. In the darkest corner of the room, there stood a lone telescope. It was covered in scratches, and dents, and just about every other sort of imperfection imaginable.

"Ah, you found it," said Silas.

Emily stared at the telescope intently. "Who did this one belong to?"

"This belonged to the first mate. It certainly doesn't give a happy image, but I believe that it is still worth looking through."

Emily pointed the telescope to the sea and looked through the lens. At first, the image caused her to jump out of shock. All of the color disappeared, the waves crashed about angrily, and a glowing gray fog sat above the sea. "Is this really how he viewed the world?" she asked.

Silas sighed, "Aye."

Inside, Emily felt sad. Her mind suddenly whooshed back

to the time when the world around her seemed nearly as colorless as the world through that telescope.

Upon seeing the melancholy in Emily's eyes, Elliott could not help but add his own thoughts to the subject. "I do feel quite bad for those who feel sad. Sadness affects them in a way that can darken up their day. But I know a secret of what sadness can do. May I share that secret with you?"

Emily nodded her head.

"When the world around you is sad, there are things that can make you glad. The rain quickly becomes a friend, and soon you hope it will never end. The gloom is friendly too, because it is similar to you."

"I never thought of it in that way, Elliott," said Emily attentively.

Elliott's sweet words also came with a bit of warning, though. "But if you introduce wrath to gloom," he added, "disaster will swiftly bloom. This is what the first mate had in mind when he became so unkind. Now his entire way of life is full of hate and full of strife."

"How do you know that?" asked Silas. "Perhaps he's changed. There is no way of knowing for sure."

Elliott remained silent. There are two different reasons for remaining silent. The first and most common reason is simply having nothing else to say. The second reason for remaining silent, though, is the fear that speaking any further on the subject will only cause more trouble. The wide-eyed look on Elliott's face told Silas that he was remaining silent precisely for the second reason. You see, Elliott knew things about the first mate that no one else knew, and he feared that if he spoke of him in detail, trouble would inescapably follow. So they remained hushed until all interest in the subject passed by (although not completely, as Emily had many questions that she wanted to ask).

By this time, the pattering of the rain ceased to hit the glassy ceiling, and the purple clouds made way for the bright moonlight. "Well, the rain has finally stopped," Silas pronounced.

"It has, hasn't it?" commented Steven, who had finally detached himself from Captain Cecil's telescope. "We still have many places to see," he added.

"Ah, that's right!" shouted Silas. "We had plans to go to the sea cave. We should by all means be on our way!"

Elliott then pressed a green button, and the four of them gathered in the middle of the room. The floor and walls swished in circles until they found themselves standing in the music box room once again (and surprisingly, none of them were the least bit dizzy).

"So! We shall board my ship and sail north to the sea cave. How does that sound?" asked Silas.

"That sounds like a wonderful plan!" said Steven.

"Good! We'd best get going now!"

During this conversation, Elliott stood near the edge of his dusty corner, and listened intently. "Would you care to go with us, dear brother?" added Silas, to which Elliott's face lit up with a smile. "Sadly, I don't think I can. I do hope you understand. If I were to leave my music box room, I would be full of gloom!"

"Dear brother, you know that I understand. I will try to visit you again soon."

Before they left, Emily could not help but compliment Elliott and his music box room, "I will never forget you or your music box room, Elliott," she said. "This has been a most fascinating visit. Will we see you again one day?"

"Yes, Elliott? May we visit you again?" added Steven.

Elliott took both of their hands, and began to speak. "I know one day we will meet again. I'm so glad you are my new friends. And I hope, quite precisely, that you will always think of me nicely."

Emily and Steven did not reply with words, but with a smile (they both feared that, if they tried to speak, tears would start to trickle). At that, the three of them left the music box room and Silas closed the door tightly before walking towards the staircase that seemed to be a bit longer than ever.

Twelve

THE CURIOUS SEA CAVE
AND THE GREAT GOLDFISH

"Would you like to know the secret of how to cut your staircase travels in half?" asked Silas.

Emily and Steven nodded at such a wonderfully odd question.

"The rails of these stairs are very special," he smiled. "They are the only rails in the world that you can slide down without falling. You just sit right on the railing, and slide like butter on toast!"

Steven admired the rails. They had a certain shininess that he could not ignore. "No one has ever fallen?" he asked skeptically.

"Never! For some unknown reason, anything that falls down this staircase floats back up before it hits the ground." As a demonstration, Silas took his most prized golden anchor-shaped pin and threw it over the railing with much force. Within a few seconds, it came floating back up to him.

"Fantastic!" cried Emily.

"Wonderful!" roared Steven.

Silas smiled at their enthusiasm. "Now, ever since I was young," he said, "I've been sliding down these rails. In fact, it's the only way I've ever gotten down. The key is to believe that all fantastic things are possible, and then just close your eyes and slide!"

Steven and Emily gazed at the rails from nearly every angle.

"Now, time is running away from us," said Silas. "We'd best get sliding!"

So, the three of them sat on the rail, and began to slide. They spun around the spirals and gained more speed with each turn. Once, Steven nearly tumbled back onto the steps, but picked himself up just in time. Emily had no problem balancing herself. She figured that if she was able to stand on a floating cloud without falling, she could balance herself on nearly anything. Round and round they spun down the horribly long staircase and, from where they sat, there seemed to be no end in sight.

"Now, could you imagine where we would be if we had decided to walk?" asked Silas with a laugh.

"Why is the staircase so long?" inquired Emily, who expected the journey down to be much shorter than the journey up.

"Perhaps it is your perspective," said Silas. "Sometimes, when we do not want to leave, but must leave, the trip back to where we started is like a thousand journeys rolled up into one."

Emily remained silent, and wondered if Silas was, in fact, correct in his words. "Well, I do believe I could have spent hours upon hours in the top of that lighthouse," she said quietly, to which Silas smiled.

Round and round they continued to spin, and soon
enough, they reached the bottom.

"Well, wasn't that fun?" asked Silas. "And we all made it
down safely. This would be a cause for celebration any other
day. Today, though, we must keep moving. Now, follow me to
my ship, and we'll be on our way!" So, Silas, Emily, and
Steven sprinted from the lighthouse, through the sand, and to
the dock. In no time at all, they found themselves standing in
front of Silas' ship as it waited for them patiently. Steven and
Emily could not help but admire it. You see, they found within
themselves a certain amazement while staring at it. It was not
the amazement that they experienced while staring into
Alcovia's sky, or listening to the leaves play their symphony.
No, this amazement was entirely different, and the only
sensible reason for such a difference was the ship's ability to
take them anywhere they pleased. In a way, that very ship
represented adventure itself, and this made Emily and Steven
incredibly excited to take a ride on it.

"What is her name?" asked Steven. From his studies of
sailors, he learned that most ships had names, and sometimes
sailors referred to their ship as simply 'her' or 'she.'

"Good question, Steven!" said Silas, obviously impressed. "I call her Pearlie the Drifter, for she never settles in one place. Ah, sweet Pearlie and I have spent many a year together. She is the dearest friend I know. It's funny how things without voices or faces or thoughts can make such good companions. And to think I built her all with my own hands. How proud she makes me!"

Emily gazed at Pearlie the Drifter and, in noticing her interest, Silas continued to speak, "She is sixty and a half feet long and weighs many tons. You know, she's even got one cannon…just in case of any disruption," he laughed. Silas spoke with so much affection for Pearlie, and gave no indication that he was bored of this subject. "I built her with the finest oak, and I polished each plank before taking her out to sea," he continued. "You should have seen it! Her glisten was brighter than the moon and stars combined! I'm afraid that now, though, the barnacles have gotten to her, and they intend to stay for a very long time. Ah, but I still love Pearlie all the same, if not more than I did on that first sail. Most sailors say that their first love is the sea, but mine is my ship. Ah, goodness me!" he gasped. "We must get going now, shouldn't we? Time always seems to stop when I talk about my favorite things." Immediately, Silas climbed up into his ship by means of a rope. A few seconds later, a tall ladder came flying down over the side. "Just climb up that ladder!" yelled Silas. "I'll be right here should you need me."

Emily and Steven stared at the ladder from top to bottom, and silently tried to decide who should climb first. "I believe I can climb it first, Steven," said Emily with a quiver of confidence. "After all, if I do happen to tumble down, at least you'll be down here to cushion my fall," she laughed. So, she stood at the foot of the ladder, looked straight up, and began to climb. The higher she climbed, the more the ladder swished back and forth.

"Is everything okay up there, Emily?" cried Steven from the dock.

"Yes, everything is fine!" she yelled in response. By this time, she was so high up that even the birds flew at the same height as her, and one even landed on her shoulder and stayed with her until she reached the inside of the ship.

"Have you made a new friend?" asked Silas while pointing at the black feathered bird, who squawked at his question.

"It looks like I have," laughed Emily.

A few minutes passed, and Steven had not finished climbing the ladder. "Where could that boy be?" said Silas, peering down to the empty dock. From the look of it, Steven had disappeared completely. "I think we've lost a member of the crew," gasped Silas.

"You really think I'm a member of your crew?" asked Steven, seemingly out of nowhere.

"How did you get up here so quick?" cried Silas.

"Oh, I just let a couple birds carry me up," he stated, as though he were describing a perfectly normal event. "It is much quicker than climbing up that silly ladder. You should try it sometime."

Silas and Emily could only stare at him quietly for a moment, unable to tell if he was joking or telling the truth. "Well! That about does it, then!" said Silas. "Now marks the beginning of our voyage! Emily, would you like to steer the ship out to sea?"

Emily giggled, "You must be joking with me. I've never sailed a ship in my life! I don't even think someone like me could steer a big ship like this."

"Ah, and what do you mean by that?" asked Silas. "You must never underestimate yourself, Emily. You may be surprised to see all that you're capable of. Now, if I'm not mistaken, I think I can faintly hear the waves calling your name and shouting for you. What do you say? Are you ready to steer Pearlie out to sea?"

Emily quivered. "Well, I don't see why I shouldn't try, at least. Will you stay beside me in case I make any mistakes?"

"Well, if I must; that is, if it will make you happy. After you, Emily!"

So, Emily stepped to the helm (which was barely reachable) and began to steer the ship away from the dock, catching a nice breeze in the sails as she did so. "Ah, well done, Emily!" cheered Silas.

"Brilliant, just brilliant!" clapped Steven.

The breeze blew through Emily's hair, and her cheeks turned pink with delight. Oh, the possibilities that suddenly danced before her! Possibilities that had never crossed her mind in the past were now impossible to ignore. Maybe she would become a sailor and explore every inch of the sea. One thing was certain: if she became a sailor, she would have to have her very own ship. It would be a glass ship with sails made out of her favorite flowery bed sheets. What a fantastic possibility! As Emily sailed, she imagined that she was behind the helm of her own make-believe ship, and she felt as though she could accomplish anything.

"Emily," said Silas. "Look at where you've taken us!"

Emily blinked her eyes tightly, and when she opened them, she saw something sparkle in the distance. "Is that...a jewel?" she asked.

"You could call it that. Many refer to it simply as the 'sea cave.'"

Emily gasped, "Did I really just sail us all the way here?"

"Aye," said Silas excitedly. "I wouldn't be surprised if you have a compass built into that head of yours! Now, it looks as though we still have a bit of time left before we are close enough to drop the anchor. Why don't you let me take over while you explore the ship? It would be wise to become familiar with the workings of a ship, in case you have one of your own someday."

"You really think so? I could own my own ship?"

"Ah, it would be a shame if your sailing skills went to waste! Now, go and explore. I highly recommend you take a look at the deck. I polished the floors the other day, and they look rather glittery. If you have anything to ask me, I'll be standing right here, sailing towards the sea cave."

So, Emily did just as Silas said, and wandered around the ship– paying much attention to the deck as she did so. She paced from one end to the other, and admired the shiny floors. Then, with no effort at all, she began to daydream once again. Through her eyes, the ship changed from wooden to glass (just as it had looked during her last daydream). The floors were completely clear, and through them, you could see straight into the ocean. What a dream it was to imagine watching the inner-workings of the sea from the middle of a ship! In her mind, Emily created a list of all the features her future ship would have. So far, the list went something like this:

1. Made entirely out of glass.

2. Strong enough to sail through a thousand storms.

3. Favorite flowery bed sheets as sails.

4. A special place for telescopes.

5. Enough room for Steven, Silas, and – hopefully — Elliott (should he ever want to leave his music box room).

This was only the beginning of her list. And even though she did not know how she would ever begin building such a majestic ship, she knew that one thing was certain: the ship would exist – even if it took years. The daydream did not stop there. Soon Emily dreamt of what she would name her ship. What an important task that would be! In fact, it was so important that it made Emily feel horribly anxious and exhausted.

"You look troubled," said Steven. "Is something the matter?"

Emily sighed, "Oh no, no, no. Nothing is wrong. I'm just thinking."

"About what?" (Steven could never resist the temptation of knowing the thoughts of others.)

"Well," said Emily, "I was thinking of how I'd design a ship of my own."

"What an interesting thing to think about. Have you got any ideas to share with me?"

"In fact, I do. I decided that the ship would be made out of glass and—"

Steven interrupted Emily's description, "How fascinating! I suppose a glass ship would only be practical. How else would you be able to view everything under the sea without getting soaked? I hope to ride that ship one day, Emily."

Emily sighed, "I hope so too."

Suddenly, the ship slowed down, and the sea cave was now close enough to touch. In person, it looked like a gigantic black jewel as it sparkled (which surpassed any expectations that Emily and Steven had).

Upon gazing, they found that the source of the sparkle was millions of diamonds encrusted in the rock. Because there were so many diamonds, Emily could not help but ask Silas why no one had taken them. "Well, Emily," he said, "would the outside of this sea cave be as beautiful if most of the diamonds were missing?"

"Oh, of course not!" replied Emily.

"And that, my dear, is the reason why no one has taken them. If people made a habit of snatching the diamonds, then not only would they be robbing the sea cave of its beauty, but they would also be robbing innocent observers of such an amazing sight!"

"Well, that makes sense now that you explain it," said Emily.

"Ah, I can manage to make sense of myself at least once in a while," laughed Silas before steering his ship into the cave.

As they made their way inside, they had an awful time seeing anything. It seemed as though the farther they went, the darker it got. Before it became impossible to see anything, though, Silas quickly lit a few lanterns. Suddenly, a bright golden glow covered each inch of the sea cave. "Surely that light isn't coming from my lanterns," cried Silas. "They are far too old to have that bright of a glow!"

"No, that light is most certainly coming from something else," said Emily shakily with her eyes fixed to something in the distance. "Silas, I think you should look over here."

"Oh my!" cried Silas upon seeing such a majestic sight.

"I've never seen anything like it in my life," mused Steven. "Could it really be?"

Silas continued to gaze, "Aye, Steven, it is."

Now by this time, you have probably concluded that the three of them have discovered the great goldfish. And, by their awed reactions, you would find that the sight of such a majestic creature left them entirely stunned (after all, how many times in life does one come across a giant, glowing goldfish in the middle of a dark, diamond-covered sea cave?). If the sight of the goldfish was not stunning enough, its glow hit hundreds of diamonds, which gave the lovely effect of sailing through the stars.

"Perhaps we should sail a bit closer to the goldfish so she will know we're here," suggested Emily. "After all, I would love to meet her."

"Ah, what a good idea, Emily!" said Silas. "That is exactly what we will do." So, Silas slowly navigated the ship towards it. As soon as the goldfish saw that a large ship was coming its way, it began to flap its fins in fright. In fact, the goldfish was so frightened that its twists and flaps caused rumbles of waves within the sea cave. Some of the waves were so fierce that they nearly knocked Steven and Emily right out of the ship.

"Hold on!" cried Silas. "We've got an angry one here!"

"I don't think it's angry!" yelled Emily with a mouth half full of water. "I think it's frightened!"

"Let's try to calm her down," added Steven.

"I have an idea," shouted Emily. "I'll dive in the water, and console the goldfish. I'm sure it will calm down if I whisper to it and introduce myself."

"How in the world will you manage that?" asked Silas.

"I'll tie rope around my wrist. If I tug on it once, then that means I need help. If I tug on it twice, then everything is okay. Understand?"

"Are you sure about this, Emily?" asked Steven.

"Entirely," she responded before jumping over the edge of the ship. As soon as she hit the water, she dove underneath the waves and swam to the goldfish. Even by this time, the goldfish had not let up in its wave-making, and Emily had a most difficult time swimming her way towards it. Eventually, she found a rock next to the goldfish, and stepped onto it. "It's okay," she whispered. "We won't hurt you one bit." The goldfish stopped to listen. "We have seen paintings of you, goldfish. Your owners were quite talented." After mentioning the paintings, the goldfish stopped all movement, and Emily wondered if it would begin to speak right back to her (she prepared herself for the oddest things to happen, of course), but instead of speaking, the goldfish swam away, and came back with a paintbrush in its mouth. Before it did anything else, Emily asked it if it would be okay for Silas and Steven to come closer, to which the goldfish responded by twirling around and fluttering its watery blue eyes (which naturally signified its approval). So, as Silas and Steven sailed nearer, the goldfish began to paint a picture on the wall of the sea cave.

"Did Florence and Laurence teach you to paint?" asked Emily.

The goldfish batted its eyes.

"I bet they were marvelous teachers. You know, I've always wanted to paint, but I've never had the patience and...oh how lovely!" when Emily caught sight of the goldfish's painting, she nearly toppled into the water. The painting clearly depicted Florence and Laurence teaching the goldfish how to paint. Laurence stood in the water with a paint palette, and Florence was giving it a paintbrush.

"Did you paint that, Emily?" asked Silas as he threw his anchor in the water.

"No, the goldfish happened to paint it," said Emily in a fascinated haze. "I think painting is how it communicates," she added in a whisper.

Steven stood at the edge of the ship with his arms crossed as he watched the goldfish finish its painting. "Is it trying to tell us more about Florence and Laurence?" he asked Emily.

"I suppose it is," she said in response. "It seems as though Florence and Laurence taught the goldfish how to paint after all. What a smart goldfish it is!"

After the goldfish finished painting, it began to swim forward through the sea cave.

"I think it wants us to follow along," said Silas. So, along with Emily and Steven, he followed close behind the goldfish. Before they knew it, they found themselves surrounded by words and paintings upon the rock. One thing that stood out the most, though, was an incredibly large painting of a grand carousel. Under the painting, a scribbled caption read:

THE LOCATION OF THE CAROUSEL'S KEY
IS KNOWN ONLY BY THE GOLDFISH

"I've heard stories of that carousel," said Silas. "My father spoke of it often. It spins around, and when it stops spinning, well, something fantastic happens."

"So it's a real place?" asked Emily.

"Aye. I've never been there, of course. It hasn't been in working order in ages."

Suddenly, the goldfish began to nudge the ship in order to get their attention. Once everyone stopped speaking, the goldfish directed their eyes to another sentence, which said:

IF THE GOLDFISH IS SHOWING YOU THIS SENTENCE,
THEN IT BELIEVES THAT YOU DESERVE
TO HAVE THE KEY

"How fantastic," laughed Steven. "Do you really want to take us to the carousel, goldfish?"

The goldfish swam in happy circles.

"Shall we follow you, then?"

The goldfish then sped through the cave and out into the open sea, hoping that her new friends would follow. Once they finally caught up, she swam quickly towards land.

"I've never seen a goldfish swim this fast!" cried Steven.

"Neither have I," agreed Emily.

"Well, now you can say you have!" exclaimed Silas from his helm.

In the distance, they could see tall mountains. If you have ever had the pleasure of seeing mountains from afar, you can probably imagine how excellent it looked (and, if you have a good imagination, perhaps you could even picture yourself there).

Soon enough, they found themselves near the shore, and the goldfish stopped swimming where the waves met the sand.

"What do you think she is going to do next?" asked Steven.

"Find the key to the carousel, I hope," answered Emily.

That is exactly what the goldfish did. She dug up a large clam from the sand. Then, she plopped the clam in the water and let it float towards the ship. It bobbed up and down until Silas caught it with a net. "What a treasure!" he crackled while cradling it in his hands.

"There it is," whispered Steven while gazing at the sparkly pink object. Before he could even try to get a closer look, though, the goldfish began to rock the ship back and forth.

"What is it, goldfish?" asked Emily.

The goldfish then waved her fin, blinked her eyes, and swam back to her sea cave before anyone had the chance to say goodbye.

"Why, I believe she wants us to keep the key!" said Steven ecstatically while gazing at the clam.

Emily scrunched up her eyes. "It seems that way, doesn't it? Do you think we should open it now?"

"Oh yes!"

So, Steven gently opened up the clam, and looked at the key. "You know," he said, "it would be very smart to use this key as soon as possible. After all, I'm sure the goldfish would have preferred it that way. Silas, do you think we could park the ship somewhere?"

Silas drew in a breath and smiled. "Well, Steven, I don't think I'll be joining you. I hope you understand. I know that soon, I'll find that world of darkness and harsh waves. It would be such a shame if I missed my opportunity."

"I understand entirely," said Emily softly. "We will meet again, won't we?"

"Ah, it would be impossible for me to forget rare treasures such as you both. We will meet again soon. I'm certain of it." Silas then went on to sail his ship as close as he could to the shore. And once Emily and Steven made it onto the sand, he began to sail away. As they watched him sail from afar for the second time, they no longer saw him as a mysterious figure, but as a dear friend. And they had no hint of sadness, because they knew that they would most certainly see him again. After he was completely out of sight, they examined their surroundings and found that they were quite easily standing in the oddest part of Alcovia yet.

Thirteen

THE INCREDIBLE CAROUSEL OF SEASONS

"I'm certain that the carousel must be around here somewhere," said Steven as he and Emily wandered around. They walked so far that the seaside eventually turned into a forest with nothing but tall, snow-covered trees surrounding them. "I thought winter only took place in Alcovia's mountains," he added.

"No, you're quite wrong about that, boy," said a wispy, unfamiliar voice that coughed after every second or third word.

"Who is there?" asked Steven, rather startled.

"Why, I'm the carousel keeper, of course." (The source of the voice remained unseen.)

"Excuse us sir, but if you don't mind, please come out from hiding so we can see you properly. I've never seen a carousel keeper in person before, but I'd imagine they are very charming." added Emily.

After saying this, a man in a ratty gray jacket appeared from behind a tree. He was rather old, and when he stood in front of the wild, snowy trees, it was difficult to tell where the branches ended and his hair began. "You must excuse my shyness," he whispered. "I may seem very unimpressed at your interest in the carousel, but on the inside, I am as warm as summertime."

"There is never a need to apologize for shyness," said Steven. "If you don't mind my asking, where would the carousel be? We have been searching for it for some time now!"

The carousel keeper gazed at the ground wistfully. "If you saw it, I'm afraid you would only find disappointment."

"Why is that?" Emily asked.

"Well, when the carousel was in working order, it was the most spectacular thing you could find in Alcovia. Since its key went missing, though, I regret to say that it is nothing but a waste of space."

Emily and Steven looked at each other, excited to tell the carousel keeper of the key that they had in their possession. "Tell me, carousel keeper, when you hear good news, do you find it difficult to keep your balance?" asked Emily with a contained smile.

"Oh yes!" he cried in response. "In fact, I find it nearly impossible!"

"Well, if that's the case, then I think you should lean up against a tree."

So, the carousel keeper did exactly as Emily suggested, and leaned up against the first tree he could find. As soon as he did so, Emily took the shiny clam out of her pocket and held it close to his glossy eyes. "What does it mean?" he asked, sounding disappointed.

"You must remember that many spectacular things hide in the most unlikely of places," said Emily before opening the clam and revealing the key to the carousel keeper, who tipped over with excitement at the very sight of it. "Are you alright?" gasped Emily as Steven helped him stand up again. The carousel keeper swiftly dusted off his jacket, and began to run frantically towards the woods.

"Please follow the key and bring me!" he cried before stopping to rephrase his sentence: "You must pardon my excitement. I meant to tell you to follow me and bring the key!"

So, Emily and Steven did their best to follow the carousel keeper as closely as possible. "I've never seen an old man run this fast in my entire life!" said Steven, spellbound.

"I must agree," added Emily. By this time, the carousel keeper was no longer in sight, and they found themselves with only his footprints to follow. The footprints soon led them directly to the carousel. What a sad sight it was! From top to bottom, it was drenched in gray. All of the horses, and kangaroos, and elephants (amongst many other animals) had no character or colors, and they sat frozen in (what seemed to be) an everlasting gloom.

"Oh, the key!" said the carousel keeper as soon as he saw that Steven and Emily had finally caught up. "Please hand me the key! Please, oh please, I beg you!"

Emily gently took the key from the clam, and handed it to the carousel keeper. "Mark my words!" he cried. "You aren't going to see anything as spectacular as this!" As soon as he turned the key with his grim, shaky hand, the carousel's lights lit up one by one, drenching the animals (and forest) in bright colors. Even the air was aglow with a fuzzy little tune that played from the old, dusty speakers. "You don't know how long I've waited for this very moment," said the carousel keeper. "I may give way to tears. If I do, you must promise not to laugh!"

Emily and Steven gazed at the carousel. Yes, it truly was a sight. The animals glistened, and on the ceiling were portraits of each season (but these were not ordinary portraits, as you will soon find out).

"What do you think?" whispered Steven to Emily.

"I think it's fantastic. Do you think he'll let us ride it?"

"Oh, I don't see why not, but I may as well ask." Steven

gently tapped the carousel keeper's shoulder, causing him to jump out of excitement.

"Oh, you want a ride!" he yelled. "Yes, take your pick of any animal, and I'll do the rest!"

"Thank you, carousel keeper! Come on, Emily, let's go!" said Steven as he stepped onto the platform. So he and Emily walked around and around a few times until they finally found the animal they wanted. Steven chose a glass pony with a silver mane and a blue saddle. And Emily chose a pink rabbit with little black rhinestones for eyes.

Once they were quite comfortable on their animals, the carousel keeper clearly stated his instructions, "Hold on tight, you'll be spinning soon. My, oh my, oh my! There's no telling what will happen next!" his voice echoed all around the carousel, which soon gave way to a moment of silence, but the carousel remained motionless. "I can't seem to find the proper moment to start it," sighed the carousel keeper, "I just can't!"

"Please take your time! We wouldn't want you to start the carousel at the wrong moment," said Emily.

So, the carousel keeper turned in circles and lifted his hands to the air. "I'm measuring the wind. You wouldn't want to spin around too fast if it is too windy – certainly not!" he said before turning in another circle. "Ah, yes! Now is the perfect time. Hold on, and keep your eyes fixed to the ceiling, if you're able to, of course!" the carousel keeper then pushed a couple of buttons, and the platform began to spin. "Why, I haven't seen it move around in years," he whispered with a tissue close to his eye. As Emily and Steven spun round and round, the paintings on the ceiling of the carousel changed. In one moment, the painting portrayed a sparkling winter day. In another moment, it transformed to a lush, green summer scene. At the very instant of that change, the carousel made a smooth stop. The carousel keeper then scattered from his seat, and quickly removed his ratty gray jacket. "Wait for it! Wait for it!" he cried. (Now, the following words may sound rather outlandish, but you must remember: anything can happen in Alcovia.) Suddenly, a wave of warmth danced through the snowy air, the leafless trees bloomed with leaves before you could even blink your eyes, and the clouds in the once-winter sky scattered away to reveal the bright, warm sun. "Do you see what happened? What phenomenon just took place?" said a chirpy man in a green velvet suit whose hair matched the color of the sun.

Emily, in a stunned tone of voice, tried her best to respond to the man, "Th-the ceiling of the carousel stopped on a picture of summer, and the season changed to match it! Oh, it is so fantastic." It was only after she stopped speaking that she realized she did not recognize whom she was speaking to, "What happened to the carousel keeper?" she asked, "I would have enjoyed watching his reaction to this!"

The man in green could only laugh for a moment. "You really are too funny, my child!" he said. "I am the carousel keeper!"

Steven looked at the man up and down. "What a clever joke!" he laughed.

"Oh no," cried the carousel keeper. "It most certainly is not a joke. I change just like the seasons do. Oh how I've longed to be like summer again. A bit of chilled air is nice, of course, but it can be so tiring to feel cold all the time. I'm all warm now, and I feel sunnier than ever! But, if you still don't believe me, I challenge you to another ride. When the season changes, just take a look at me and I'll be changing too!"

So Steven hopped onto his pony, and Emily climbed back onto her rabbit, and the carousel spun once again. This time around, it landed on autumn. As expected, a phenomenon took place: the summertime air, trees, and sky changed. Leaves drenched in vibrant shades of red and orange clothed the trees and clouds blanketed the sky. Even the temperature of the air shifted from warm to chilly. This barely phased Emily and Steven as they kept their eyes fixed to the carousel keeper, who stood still as his green velvet suit turned to a toasty shade of corduroy, and his sunny blonde hair turned brown. "Do you believe me now?" he asked calmly (his voice sounded remarkably similar to the crisp autumn breeze).

Emily and Steven looked at each other in agreement. "Yes, we believe you now," said Steven.

"But, how do you change so quickly?" added Emily.

The carousel keeper laughed, "I've been asking myself the same question for years. Some things are better left unknown, I suppose. Now tell me, isn't this carousel the most magnificent thing you've ever seen?"

"I think it's incredible!" stated Emily. "Of course, I would have to say that I'm glad seasons don't change like this in the rest of Alcovia. Could you imagine never being able to tell which season was going to come next?"

The carousel keeper's face lit up, "That is exactly what I wanted to hear you say, dear Emily. This carousel is not only incredible, but it is also a reminder – a reminder to enjoy the seasons as they come and go. I don't think it could get any more inspiring. In fact, I was so inspired that I wrote a poem. Would you mind hearing me recite it?"

"Oh, not at all!" said Steven.

"We would love to hear it," added Emily.

So, the carousel keeper smiled, drew in a breath, and began to recite his words:

"Nothing is lovelier than a season:
Winter, spring, summer, and fall.
And for many different reasons,
I happen to love them all.
Winter for its dark blanket
That covers up the sky
And for its icy snowflakes
That dance as they float on by.
Spring for its pretty flowers
Thriving in cool, clear rain.
Summer for its playful days

And evening walks down the lane.
Fall for its lovely trees
Dressed up in orange and red.
And for its cool air
(That helps clear up the head).
I love many things about the seasons
As you can clearly see.
And I could list one-hundred more
But you may feel quite bored with me!"

"*Are* you bored?" asked the carousel keeper abruptly.

Emily and Steven both assured him that they weren't.

"Oh good!" he cried. "Then I shall keep on going!"

"But I love the in-between days, too
When the summer moons are blue
And when the stars light up the sky
Just like a familiar passerby.
Oh, and when the wind blows through the air
I cannot help but smile
Because it reminds me of days so fair
And I forget everything that's vile.
There are so many vile things, you know,

And it really is quite tremendous
To find something that erases
Thoughts of something horrendous—"

In the middle of the carousel keeper's recitation, Steven had a terrible urge to yawn. If you have ever had such an urge, you would know exactly what Steven was going through. After a few moments of struggling, he could not help but give in to his urge. As soon as the carousel keeper saw him, he stopped speaking. "Oh, you are bored!" he cried. "I could tell by the way you yawned. Oh dear, oh dear, whatever shall we do now?" By this time, the carousel keeper paced back and forth swiftly, just like a windy autumn night. "You know, I wanted to ask you where you found the key in the first place. That is, if you can remember…"

"Well," said Emily, "we visited the sea cave, and the goldfish directed us to the key. It's quite simple, really."

Upon hearing this information, the carousel keeper jumped back. "You must be joking!" he yelled. "I can't believe that goldfish still lives in the sea cave."

"You know the goldfish?"

"As well as anyone would, I suppose. You see, the goldfish used to keep me company— that is, until I gave her to the twins as a prize. A long time ago, I made a game out of this carousel. Along the sides, I set up pots of flowers, and if you picked at least three flowers while staying seated on your animal, you'd get a prize. Incidentally, Florence and Laurence finished with a bouquet!"

"But, how did the goldfish end up with your key?" asked Emily.

The carousel keeper sighed bashfully. "When you have a friend, you try to do all you can to make them happy. For the longest time, I had the awful habit of shutting the carousel down when it wasn't in use, and leaving the key next to the goldfish's bowl. Well, one day, I noticed her gazing at the key, and I asked her if she'd like a closer look. Oh, how she spun at the very idea of it! So, like any good friend, I plopped the key in her bowl, and I would leave it with her until the next ride. When I gave her to Florence and Laurence as a prize for my game, I didn't realize I was giving them the key to my beloved carousel, too!" After the carousel keeper explained how his key went missing, there was a moment of silence. That is, until, a marvelous idea struck him. "Funnily enough," he laughed, "you remind me of the twins. I wonder if you could also – oh, it's too silly to even think about!"

"What? What were you going to say?" asked Steven.

"Well, I was going to see if you could try the game and beat the twins' record. Oh, but that's a terrible idea, because it's autumn now, and there aren't any flowers blooming."

"Why don't we ride the carousel until we land on springtime?" suggested Emily.

The carousel keeper kept his eyes fixed to the ground. "You could try, but that could take hours, perhaps even decades."

"Then we'd best get started now!" cried Steven in the midst of sprinting back to his glass pony. Emily followed close behind him. As soon as they both found their animals, the carousel keeper anxiously pressed the button that made the carousel move. Inside, his autumn heart pounded, and he wondered how long it would be before he would see the flowers of springtime again. On the first stop, the carousel landed on winter, but before the snowflakes could hit the ground, the carousel keeper pressed the button again. This time, though, the carousel rotated for a few seconds until it landed on a little gray sliver of a picture. Then it spun backwards, then forwards, then backwards without stopping.

"My, my, that's not supposed to happen. How horribly odd," whispered the carousel keeper to himself. Before he could even think of pressing the big, ruby red STOP button, his eyes were already fixed on the back and forth motions of the carousel. How fascinating it was! In the midst of it all, Emily and Steven held on tight to their animals, and wondered why the carousel keeper took so long to stop the ride.

"Please, carousel keeper, you must stop the ride! We're getting dizzy!" cried Steven with his eyes closed tight.

The sound of Steven's voice interrupted the carousel keeper's concentration. "Oh yes, oh yes!" he said while scrambling to press the STOP button. "Don't worry; I'm pressing the stop button right now—oh dear, why isn't it working?" Now, as you can imagine, the carousel keeper was utterly frantic. As he stood at the circuit board, he stared at the buttons, wondering why none of them did their job. "I wasn't trained for this!" he cried. "Oh no, oh no, whatever shall I do now?" His hands shook and his heart thumped; what if the carousel never stopped? Before he could think of more scary things, his memory struck him. Underneath the circuit board, he remembered an old dusty book entitled "WHAT TO DO IF

THE CAROUSEL MISBEHAVES." As he reached for the book, his hands continued to shake. In fact, they shook so quickly, that he could barely read the words written on the pages! "Just a moment!" he yelled to Steven and Emily, who continued to hold on tightly to their animals. The carousel keeper flipped through the pages, passing chapters with titles such as, "THE FLYING CAROUSEL (DON'T PANIC)" and "HOW TO HANDLE AN EVERLASTING WINTER." Eventually, near the very end of the book, he found the exact chapter he needed. It was quite a short chapter, but it said so much. It was simply entitled, "WIND" which was followed by only a few sentences that said:

"If the carousel lands on a picture of Shade Day (or, more recognizably, a little gray sliver), please stay calm. There is a black button underneath the platform, and pushing it is the only way to cease the carousel's unpredictable spins. Before creeping, crawling, or sneaking under the moving platform, please be aware that attempting such a feat could result in indescribable injury such as…"

Now, with a wave of fear, the carousel keeper stopped reading the book. He did not want to allow the carousel to spin around forever, and he certainly did not want to be injured. Yet, amidst his fear, he could vaguely see Emily and Steven anxiously hoping for their ride to end– how awful they must have felt while spinning around and around with no slowing down! Such a miserable sight was enough to give him the bravery to march tall and courageous to the unruly carousel and crawl under its platform. Now, as you can imagine, such a task was nothing short of terrifying. From under that fast-moving platform, he dodged loose springs and other things that could catch onto his clothes and cause much damage. Finally, he was able to press the black button, prompting the entire carousel to stop in its tracks. And, when he managed to crawl out from under the paralyzed platform, he was shocked to find that it was springtime!

"Marvelous!" he shouted. "And I managed to do all that without one loose spring catching on to my trousers! ...Oh, my trousers!" As the carousel keeper spoke, his outfit changed from autumn to spring. "I haven't been like spring in a long while. What a lovely change." His jacket turned to the color of grass, and his trousers were bright pink like a flowerbed. Around his neck, he wore a gray scarf (to match the rainy sky), and his shoes sparkled like raindrops. As this marvelous change took place, Emily and Steven had finally gotten off their animals, but they were still unable to walk. "Now!" said the carousel keeper as he looked to Steven and Emily excitedly. "Let me go grab a few bouquets of flowers, and you can play the game!"

Once the carousel keeper ran off into a nearby garden, Steven and Emily looked at each other wearily. "I can't even look at this carousel, let alone take another ride!" stated Emily (who had briefly considered leaving the carousel keeper a nice note saying that she and Steven had somewhere they needed to be). In no time at all, though, the carousel keeper came running back to them, up to his nose in the flowers that he carried.

"Ah, the flowers are simply beautiful," he proclaimed. "I cannot wait to see how many you can catch as you're riding this marvelous carousel!" He spoke so happily, almost as though he completely forgot the chaos that took place only a few minutes before. "Oh, what ARE you waiting for?" he shouted as he waited for Emily and Steven to climb onto their animals once again.

"But we are still so dizzy!" said Steven from the platform.

At once, the carousel keeper jumped onto the platform, "I have a cure for that!" he said. "First, you must tilt your head to the left, then to the right. Once you've done that, spin around once with your eyes closed."

"You mean we have to spin around even more?" asked

Emily.

"Yes, if you want to stop your dizziness. Just try it."

So, Steven and Emily slowly tilted their dizzy little heads to the left, then to the right. By this time, their dizziness was halfway gone. Then they moved on to the most difficult part– or so they thought. At first, they hesitated a bit. After all, if you're dizzy, why spin even more? Still, they had no other choice. So they braced themselves and did a short little spin with their eyes tightly shut.

"Now!" shouted the carousel keeper. "Your dizziness is gone, isn't it?"

Slowly, Steven opened his eyes, and much to his happiness, the dizziness was gone! "Emily, open your eyes," he shouted, "I promise you won't be dizzy anymore!" So, Emily opened one eye at a time, and was elated to find that her dizziness had also vanished. "I don't understand. Why did spinning around in circles get rid of the dizziness?"

"Simply put, my dear child, it confuses the brain! Now, please, let's play the game. If you win, I will give you a wonderful prize." Now, it is a common fact that we find ourselves much more inclined to do something if there is a prize involved. For example, ANYONE would be thrilled to make their bed in the morning if they knew that a plate of warm pancakes was the prize for doing so. And how much easier it would be to clean up your room if you knew that you'd be going to the park, simply because you put your toys away! Now, this was a similar case for Emily and Steven. You see, they did not know what they would be getting as a prize, and their curiosity could not allow them to pass up such an offer. So, with a small bit of reluctance, they climbed aboard their animals and waited for the carousel to spin once again. At first, it spun slowly, and Emily was able to pick flower after flower, until she could not hold any more. Once it sped up a bit, Steven went on to grab at least three bouquets' worth! Overall, the entire thing was a bit of a blur for Emily and Steven, and before they knew it, the ride was over.

"Let's see how the both of you fared!" pronounced the carousel keeper as he put his magnifying glasses on (he took flower counting terribly seriously). "One, two, three, four...amazing! Simply amazing."

"How did we do?" shouted Emily.

"Do we get a prize?" asked Steven.

"Why, you beat the twins' record by a thousand per cent! Incredible, unbelievable, implausible! Of course you get a prize!" Suddenly, the carousel keeper disappeared into the woods, and when he came back, he held a small indigo box, secured by a purple ribbon. "There is a note inside the box explaining exactly what's inside." Just as Emily and Steven were about to reply, they were interrupted by a lovely chirping sound coming from the sky. And when they looked straight up, they were shocked to see what flew above them.

Fourteen

THE REDBIRDS APPEAR

"Well, they haven't visited me in a while," commented the carousel keeper as he glanced to the sky unenthusiastically. You see, just above their heads flew a great flock of redbirds (which, if you remember, strangely resembled the redbird painted upon Emily's front door back home). Now, you're probably thinking of how unusual a redbird must be. In Alcovia, though, they are rather common, and it is a well-known fact that their feathers are red because they eat nothing but strawberries and rose petals.

"Oh, they are magnificent!" Emily mused as the birds flew around, making different shapes in the sky. First, they made the shape of a strawberry, then of a flower. It did not take long before one of the birds noticed Emily's amazement, and perched upon her shoulder. "Hello bird, how are you today?" she asked laughingly.

"Why, how kind of you to ask!" commented the bird in reply. "I'm doing quite fine, quite fine. I don't think I've met you before, what's your name?"

"My name is Emily. What is your — wait, I didn't know birds could speak!"

The bird fluttered, "So you mean to say that, wherever you're from, birds don't chirp and tweet?"

"Well, they do that but—"

"Oh, so they do speak! You had me frightened for a moment!" said the bird with relief.

"Where I come from, though, the birds sing, not exactly speak."

"Emily, I trust you already knew all the tweeting and chirping sounds us birds make are actually deep, meaningful conversations about the weather!" stated the bird.

The carousel keeper shook his head in agreement, "I can appreciate that type of conversation!" he said.

"So…all birds talk about is the weather?" asked Emily.

"For the most part, that is what we speak to one another about! With weather, there is always something lovely to talk about! For example, if it's a sunny day, you can have a long talk about all you can do in the sun! Or if it's raining, you can talk about all the pretty flowers that will soon bloom. I would say that makes for a wonderful conversation, wouldn't you?"

"I guess I would!" giggled Emily.

Suddenly, another bird perched onto Steven's shoulder and gazed at his (nearly white) blonde hair. "How did your feathers get so white?" asked the bird.

Steven thought for a moment until he came to a reasonable conclusion. "Because I think too much," he stated.

Next, the bird peered into his pale blue eyes. "And your eyes. How did they get so blue?"

Again, Steven thought for a reasonable answer. "Oh, the same reason, I suppose. I spend all my time thinking!"

Now, by this time, Steven and Emily found themselves rather anxious to get to their next destination. You see, they absolutely had to visit the baker before the opera, so they could bring Falsetto his opera cake (and they did not want to even imagine what would happen if they arrived late). So, in his most polite voice, Steven announced that they had somewhere that they needed to be.

"Please! Let me and my friends take you to your destination," said the redbird on Emily's shoulder. "We can take you wherever you need to be in no time at all."

Emily and Steven glanced at one another, each with adventure in their eyes.

"Okay!" said Steven. "Would you mind taking us to the bakery?"

The redbird flew around gleefully. "Of course not!"

Before the birds could grab Emily and Steven, the carousel keeper rushed to say goodbye. "You have no idea how happy you've made me," he said. "Having my carousel back for these short moments has made my life brighter. Now, please, let me give you back the key."

"The key is yours!" cried Steven. "But you need to promise Emily and me one thing: whenever we visit you again, you mustn't let that carousel spin out of control!"

The carousel keeper laughed, and, while shaking their hands, remembered something very important: "Oh, and please don't forget to wait until you're back on the ground to look into the box I gave you!" he cried. In that same moment, the redbirds flocked around Steven and Emily, grabbing their sleeves with their claws, and lifting them slowly into the sky. Once they made it into midair, they could see the forest from a different perspective. The treetops looked like a garden, and the top of the carousel strangely had the warning: "BEWARE OF THE WINDS" written boldly on top of it. They swooshed and swirled through the sky, until finally, the birds landed directly in front of the bakery.

"Here we are, safe and sound," chirped the bird. "I am so glad my friends and I could help you both. We will make sure to see you again soon! But for now, the skies look like snow, and we must gather strawberries before they freeze!"

Emily and Steven thanked them and waved goodbye, until the entire flock flew out of sight.

Fifteen

HOW TO BAKE AN OPERA CAKE

"I didn't expect it to look like this," commented Steven as he looked at the outside of the bakery. If you've ever seen a bakery before, it is likely that it was small and quaint with windows full of cakes and pies. Maybe the air around the bakery even smelled like sugary syrup or toasted marshmallows. This bakery was entirely different though. On the outside, the bricks were slightly cracked, and the steely doors were tall with small round windows so high that you could barely see through them.

"Are you sure this is the bakery?" asked Emily, examining the ground for clues in the form of cookie crumbs or lollipop sticks.

"It must be!" shouted Steven, who kept jumping high in order to see through the windows, and once he finally reached them, he found relief at what he saw. "I see...oh yes! I saw a cake – pink frosting and all!" Without saying another word, he crept inside the bakery, hoping that Emily would follow.

As you may have expected, the bakery was just as odd on the inside as it was on the outside. At first glance, you'd easily think that you were standing inside a hospital. For example, little pink cakes sat on little white beds. And around the room, there were a few curtains that partitioned it. And from top to bottom, everything was bright and clean. From behind one of the curtains, you could vaguely see the outline of a tall man, who seemed to be giving a cupcake a shot of some sort.

"Do you think that's the baker?" whispered Emily while watching the man intently.

"Oh, it would just have to be," replied Steven. "Maybe I'll make a bit of noise to see if he responds."

Steven inspected the room until he found a drawer full of little silver spoons, and decided to make a quick, clanking sound with two of them. Immediately after doing so, the outline of the man moved, and the movement was soon accompanied by a voice, "I'll be with you in a moment," said the voice in a concentrating tone. "I just have to finish injecting this cupcake with blueberry filling."

"Yes, I am nearly certain it's the baker," whispered Steven, nodding.

Suddenly, the silhouette disappeared for a moment, and after a few seconds, both Steven and Emily felt a tapping on their shoulder. "You needed to speak to me?" asked a man in a long white coat

Steven gazed at the man for a moment. He was incredibly tall, with tired eyes, and violet-gray hair. "Yes, we are looking for the baker. You see, we have a very important thing to discuss with him."

The man smiled (only halfway, though), "Young man, I am the baker. What do you need help with?" The baker kept his speech impeccably formal. You see, he had not seen a new customer for a very long time, and he almost forgot how to interact with them.

"Well," sighed Steven, "we have an opera to go to, and we must bring the singer a certain kind of cake."

The baker's eyes widened, and his heart pounded. "An opera cake! You need an opera cake, don't you?"

"That's exactly what we need!" gasped Emily. "How did you know?"

"It's the baker's instinct, obviously. Now, to create such a cake, we must go to the Opera Cake Room. Please, follow me." In a rush, he hurried down the hallway, expecting Steven and Emily to follow. Even though they tried to follow him closely, they kept finding themselves sidetracked over the oddities in that bakery. For example, one room titled "INJURY ROOM" was full of cookies that spent a few minutes too long in the oven. And in another room, a pie sat on a chair with an IV bag labeled "CHOCOLATE CUSTARD (for filling)". After they passed these rooms, they made a few turns, and found themselves face to face with a vast painting that covered the entire wall. It seemed to depict the baker smiling with his creations. What a difference from the way he looked now!

"I know there are many things to look at," he commented upon noticing Emily and Steven's distraction, "but we must make haste!" So, without examining the painting further, the three of them made their way through the hall until they reached a door with a sign that boldly stated:

OPERA CAKE ROOM
For the making of opera cakes ONLY.
PLEASE PROCEED

As soon as the baker opened the glittering glass door, a certain mood overtook him, and his glum disposition vanished quickly. "What do you think of my Opera Cake Room?" he shouted.

Emily and Steven took a quick glance at the silver walls, and chandeliers made of spoons. They even took a moment to immerse themselves in the scent of toasted sugar and melted chocolate. "I've never seen or smelled anything lovelier," replied Emily.

Without responding, the baker walked back and forth with his hand on his head, as though he was deep in thought. "Before we even begin to bake a perfect opera cake," he said, "I must make sure that the both of you are thoroughly acquainted with this intricate kitchen." He began to point out different objects within the room, focusing first on some sort of oven-like contraption (which happened to look more like a miniature stage). "This is the Opera Cake Oven!" stated the baker. "I designed it myself. It is my very own creation. As you can see, it's fashioned after an actual stage because an opera cake could never bake properly in any silly old oven."

As he continued to ramble on about different reasons why opera cakes don't bake well in normal ovens, Emily and Steven could not help but find themselves captivated by the inside of the Opera Cake Oven and its lovely features (which caused the baker's words to sound terribly muffled, as words usually sound when you're not listening to them intently). You see, the walls and lighting of the oven were very dramatic. It depicted a lake at midnight and the lighting was a vibrant shade of blue.

"The blue light provides the perfect kind of heat for such a delicate cake. If the light were red, the cake would burn to a crisp. If the light were white, the cake would scarcely bake at all. It's really quite funny, but in my early days of baking, I accidentally tried to bake an opera cake in a normal, standard, or otherwise boring oven and it turned out to be terrible! It took me years to perfect this oven. Years and years and years."

Once again, the baker's words turned into muffled noises for Emily and Steven, who could not keep their eyes from wandering around that little oven. "Sorry for my rambling on. There are just so many reasons why a normal oven doesn't work for perfectly seamless opera cakes. Now if you're ready, let's move on to the next important aspect of this room," continued the baker as he walked to a table that was prepared perfectly with mixing spoons, bowls, one cake pan and a sparkling silver tray that held many different bottles. "This is the mixing area - which is a very important area," stated the baker. "You see, when you mix all the ingredients, you must do it with pure concentration. In addition, the ingredients, mixing spoons, bowls, and cake pans must be of the finest kind - or else the opera cake will not be perfect. I believe that's all I wanted to show to you before we got started. Let's see…Steven, can you hand me the mixing spoon all the way on the left please?" So, in a strange rush, Steven found an unusually large mixing spoon that sat all the way to the left of the table and handed it to the baker. "Thank you, Steven," said the baker, staring down at the counter. "Emily! Can you carefully hand me the silver tray with all of the bottles, please?" In an overly careful way, Emily grabbed each handle of the tray and placed it on the counter slowly, so as not to accidentally spill anything. "Thank you very much! If you don't mind, I'm going to do all of the mixing, but I'll let the both of you do the most important part, which is pre-heat the oven. In order to do this, you must turn the silver dial until it says 'BRAVO.' Do you think I can trust you to do that?"

By this time, Steven and Emily realized how important that oven was to the baker, so when he asked them to do such an important job, they could not help but feel a bit nervous. After all, what in the world would they do if they turned the switch and it broke, or if they accidentally pressed a button that caused the oven to fall apart (provided there was a button that did such a thing)?

"Have you preheated the oven yet?" asked the baker anxiously. Without answering, Emily quickly turned the dial, and hoped that she did so correctly. Suddenly, the blue lights flickered and flashed, leaving Steven and Emily startled.

"Is it supposed to do that?" asked Steven nervously, as though he had committed a terrible crime.

"Oh yes," replied the baker dazedly, gazing at the golden cake batter as he poured it slowly into the pan.

After the lights stopped flashing in the oven, a sweet little tune began to play, and its walls sparkled in a vibrant shade of pink. "And this," said the baker, "is our cue. Now, if you don't mind, you may open the doors to the oven." So, this is exactly what Emily and Steven did. They opened the doors carefully until the baker had the little golden opera cake situated perfectly inside the oven. "And now we wait," he whispered to himself while admiring his creation through the glass, as though it would perform some magnificent act as it baked. After staring at it for a few more seconds, an idea struck the baker, "How would you like to test a few pieces of candy?" he asked, to which Steven and Emily nodded happily. So, the baker left the room for a moment, and returned with a silver platter, covered in red candies. "The last people to try this candy were my children. Oh how they loved it!" the baker said. "Having you both here to help me bake this opera cake has reminded me of just how much I miss my dear Florence and Laurence."

At first, neither Steven nor Emily had the faintest idea of what to say to the baker, for it was a subject that he held dear to his heart and they did not want to say something that would cause him to feel even sadder. After trudging through a few moments of silence, though, Emily thought of the perfect thing to say. "We saw Florence and Laurence's paintings at the museum," she said as the candy swirled around her mouth. Before she could add how impressive the paintings were, the baker's sadness disappeared in the blink of an eye.

"Oh yes!" he cried. "They were the finest painters I had ever known. They even painted the picture on the hallway wall that you both were admiring earlier."

"I figured they did," commented Steven. "We saw their other paintings in the sea cave, as well. Oh! And it was remarkable to see how they taught the goldfish how to paint."

Suddenly, the baker jumped from his seat. "You met the goldfish?" he asked, causing a loud echo throughout the room.

"Yes, we did," said Emily. "And she is the most fantastic goldfish I have ever seen."

"Did she reveal anything interesting?" the baker inquired.

Steven and Emily thought for a moment, until Emily remembered the painting of the carousel on the sea cave wall. As soon as she made mention of it, the baker jumped out of his seat and paced the room. "And did you go to the carousel?" he asked, still pacing, with his eyes shut tight, as though he were bracing himself for something.

"We couldn't help but go," said Steven calmly. "It just sounded so interesting, and interesting it was! In fact, the goldfish led us there."

The baker's face turned pale. "And you took a ride on this carousel?"

"A few rides, actually. At one point, the carousel got stuck on Shade Day, and the poor old carousel keeper had to crawl right under the platform to stop it!"

"Shade Day!" cried the baker, causing another echo. "Please tell me what happened."

"It's quite a funny story, really. The carousel keeper wanted us to land on springtime so flowers could grow and we could play a game," explained Steven. "So, we kept riding and riding until the carousel landed on Shade Day and spun out of control. After he fixed it, we finally landed on spring, and he still wanted us to play the game. Even though we could barely move because of the dizziness, we played the game and won a little box with a prize. That reminds me! Emily and I haven't looked to see what was inside."

The baker's eyes reached the size of an abnormally round

chocolate chip cookie. "Please, you must open it at once! You must!"

At this point, both Steven and Emily sensed that the baker knew something they didn't. So, they scrambled to open the box, which revealed the shiniest golden key that they had ever seen. Upon seeing the key, the baker took in a nervous breath. "Please, follow me," he said in a crackled whisper. Once the baker left the room, Steven and Emily followed him until they reached a small yellow door covered in paint splatters (which looked terribly out of place against the sparkling clean walls).

"May I have that key?" asked the baker, still speaking in a whisper. When Steven held out the key, the baker hesitated for a moment, then took the key from Steven's hand and used it to unlock the door.

Sixteen

The Abandoned Room

The door cracked rigidly as the baker tried to pry it open. "I may need a bit of help," he said while leaning heavily against the door. After watching him for a few moments, Steven and Emily joined in. As soon as they did so, the door swung open, causing the three of them to tumble onto the ground and into the room. At first, the room was dark, which was quite exciting because the darkness always has something to reveal.

Once they all stood up, the baker turned on a light that

caused the room to go from black to bright yellow. "This was their room," he said softly while gazing at the dried-up paint palettes and the half empty glasses of pear juice. The paint was an indication that he was speaking of Florence and Laurence. Along the walls there were many paintings on display, most of which depicted the sea, the bakery, and the goldfish. And in one corner of the room there was a large green box, covered in gray dust.

"I can't get near that box," stated Steven.

"Why not?" asked the baker.

Steven sniffled. "I can handle a little dust, but that much tickles my nose and makes me sneeze!"

"What a shame. I have the same problem. Emily, do you have an allergy to dust?"

Emily nodded her head sadly; she had an allergy to dust as well.

"Well," stated the baker, "one of us must open that box, and I suppose it shall be me." So, without saying another word, he crept up to the green box and opened it swiftly, causing all of the dust to shimmy around the room. Before he could thoroughly gaze at the contents of the box, he sneezed with much force. Now, if you have an allergy to dust (or anything else that makes you sneeze and sniffle) then you will fully understand what the poor baker was going through. Throughout his sniffles, though, he examined the contents of the box. First, he pulled out a few sheets of wrinkled paper full of wonderfully messy drawings. After taking a wistful sigh, he stared at them. "These are their first drawings, and perhaps their most important," he said. "The first realizations of our talents are always the most important."

After this, there was nothing but silence as the baker tenderly sifted through the contents of that green box. Occasionally, he'd stop to take a look at something of precious importance. Other times, he'd close his eyes and sigh or smile. He repeated these motions every few minutes– that is, until his eyes fell upon something that struck the very root of his curiosity. You see, nearly every person who has ever lived has kept something of much importance in a safe place. For example, your great uncle may keep his favorite snacks locked away in an unsuspecting cabinet, or your grandmother may keep her favorite sweaters at the darkest corner of her closet. In both cases, neither the snacks nor sweaters would stand a chance at getting snatched. Now, as you can imagine, Florence and Laurence realized, from a terribly young age, that the most important of things must hide in the perfect places. So they acted upon this realization, and hid their very important thing underneath piles of papers and paints in an average old box with the hope that no one would ever find it. By now, your mind is probably jumping all around trying to figure out what they could have hidden. From the very bottom of the dusty box, the baker pulled out a tiny, water-stained map that barely covered his hand.

"How strange," he whispered to himself quietly. "Why, I've never seen this map before." He gazed at it sideways, backwards, and every other way imaginable as Emily and Steven watched intently. "I never knew that they drew a map."

"Where does it lead to?" inquired Emily; her excitement was nearly unbearable.

The baker didn't answer. The entire idea of it sent a tremble through his fingers. Still, he kept gazing. Eventually, he handed the map over to Emily and Steven, who found themselves awestruck at what they held in their hands. The front side of the paper was a map from the bakery to forest, and on the back, there were handwritten instructions, which said:

MAP TO THAT SILLY OLD TREE

(Discovered by Florence and Laurence)

Take one left.
Twelve steps ahead. Stop.
Run as fast as you can through forest.
Turn right three times in a row.
Silly old tree should be to the left.
(If it isn't, repeat the instructions.)

"Do you know what to make of it?" asked the baker.

"I believe so," whispered Steven. "There is only one hollow tree in Alcovia, making it quite a rare sight. It seems as though this is the tree that the twins were talking about."

The baker's eyes widened. "Oh yes, I do remember them talking about that tree. How odd. How horribly odd. Then again, my children always loved oddities. It doesn't surprise me one bit that they would draw a map to such things."

Before they could say anything else, RING! The alarm on the Opera Cake Oven went off loudly, beckoning the baker. "We need to take the cake out of the oven straight away!" he yelled from the hallway.

"What do you want us to do with the map?" asked Steven, still holding it in his hands.

In an echo, the baker replied, "You can keep it. Think of it as a gift from me."

Steven gently folded it up, and he and Emily made their way to the Opera Cake Room. From the outside of the door, they could hear the baker bustling all around. When they walked inside, they were not surprised to see him standing in complete concentration as he slowly iced the little golden cake.

"Shh," he said in between strokes. "This type of work must be done in complete silence." Steven and Emily simply leaned up against the wall as he stroked the sparkly spatula back and forth across the cake. At least one time, Steven sniffled (from all of the dust that he was exposed to earlier), which caused the baker to fumble a bit. And on at least two instances, Emily moved her feet in a way that made the floor crack, which again interrupted the silence. Finally, he ran out of frosting. "Perfect!" he cried. "This cake is frosted to perfection. Now! Where is that little tin...?" He looked all around the room for the perfect tin for his perfect cake.

"Could it be this one?" asked Steven, pointing to a shiny

object on the highest shelf in the room.

"Precisely!" cried the baker who, by this time, moved faster than ever. In no time at all, he carefully placed the little cake in its little tin. "Now, if this cake even touches the ground, it will turn into a thin dust. This cake isn't like any other cake, you see. It is the most fragile type of cake in existence. In fact, I can't properly explain how fragile it really is. To be honest, it's best you don't know. If you knew, then you'd be too careful, and we all know that when someone is too careful, they are far more likely to– oh what am I saying? I know you'll take my instructions very seriously. Emily, I'd like for you to be in charge of it. You seem less likely to fall." The baker slowly handed the tin over to Emily, whose hands shook at the very thought of being near it. "Now," he continued as he led them to the front door, "do you know where to go from here?"

Steven peeked outside and his nose turned red from the snowy air. In the distance, he could faintly see a tall, white mountain. "I've been to the opera house once. To get there, we need to climb to the top of that mountain..."

"Exactly. And I see that the both of you are without coats. Give me one second." In a mysterious way, he left the room, and returned with two coats: one was red, and one was green.

"These belonged to Florence and Laurence. Oh, how they loved these little coats! I think you will, too." So the baker gave the red coat to Steven, and the green coat to Emily. Once they finished putting them on, the baker sighed: "You remind me of Florence and Laurence. I can see that same sense of adventure in your eyes. Now, go on! You must make sure you deliver that cake in time!"

Steven and Emily smiled and thanked the baker for the coats. "We'll see you again soon," they said before making their way towards that tall, snowy mountain.

Seventeen

THE OPERA

"I've never felt so small in my entire life," said Emily as she and Steven gazed at the daunting mountain that stood before them. From where they stood, they could faintly see Falsetto's silver theater glistening through the fog and they could not wait to make it to the top. Now, if you have ever found yourself with the incredible task of trekking up a mountain, you would know exactly how Steven and Emily felt. If you haven't, though, I'm sure your imagination will provide you with a vivid idea of how tiring it would be. As soon as they began their journey, it started to snow, and the higher they got the faster the little snowflakes fell.

"I'm so glad that the baker gave us these coats, but I wish he had also given us gloves," said Steven before slipping his hands into his pockets. As soon as he did so, his left hand met a crumpled-up piece of paper. "What could this be?" he whispered while snatching the paper from out of his pocket. He then smoothed it up against his arm. Once the paper was completely flat, he found that it carried a most interesting list:

ODD THINGS HAPPENING ALL AT ONCE:

1. *Fast-falling snow*
2. *Gray flowers flickering once each second*
3. *Temperatures getting colder and colder*
4. *Sky darker than night*
5. *Loud wind picking up speed*
6. *Trees turning brighter and br--*

"Steven?" said Emily with much alarm in her voice, "I don't think this is supposed to happen…"

As soon as he looked up from the paper, he found that he and Emily stood in the middle of a bed of flowers that flickered once per second, just as the list described. In no time at all, the wind started to race through the hills and trees. Immediately after that, the sky grew gray and the air turned to frost.

"Emily! Do you know what this means?" he shouted, with a cloud of steam following each word. "It means that another Shade Day is on its way, and if we don't get to the opera house and warn everyone, we'll be stuck right in the middle of it! Here, look at this list. I believe it was written right before Florence and Laurence went missing!"

Now, as soon as Emily finished reading the list, she looked Steven in the eye. It was in that moment that they both realized exactly what they must do: run. Run to the opera house as fast as they could. So through the ice and through the trees, they ran and ran against the wind that whipped about in its anger. By the time they were halfway up the mountain, the violet sky had nearly become black, and the snow blurred everything around them. To make matters worse, the wind was so violent that it ripped twigs and leaves from the trees, and used them to smack Steven and Emily all around. All of this, of course, made for a terribly unpleasant journey. In the not-so-far foggy distance, though, a crystalline figure glowed and the both of them ran towards it as fast as they possibly could through such tremulous circumstances. At some points, Emily feared that the wind would whisk her away to an unknown, shadowy part of the forest. At other points, she believed that it made her run faster than ever. Either way, she could not help but find herself enjoying a (nearly) aimless run accompanied by an equal amount of fear and excitement, and she was also proud of herself for being able to run without dropping the opera cake that she held tightly in her hands.

Now, Steven resented the fact that he could not simply fly to the opera house; that is, until a wonderful idea fell upon him. From underneath the collar of his shirt, he tugged at the thin chain that held his little golden whistle. "Emily!" he cried through the howling wind, "I have an idea!"

"What is it?" she asked in a breathy voice, half running and half walking.

"Hurry up and take my hand!"

Immediately after she did so, Steven used his whistle to call down a cloud. As this cloud descended towards them, it swirled and swished all around in the wind. As soon as the both of them jumped on, the fluffy cloud took them high above ground where the air was calm and the sky held its violet hue.

"I'm sure that storm is almost over by now," sighed Steven.

"After all, how could it possibly be worse than it already was?" In the exact moment of his speaking, the cloud zigzagged sharply all around the sky.

"What was that for, silly cloud?"

The cloud twirled around in circles.

"Do you think it is trying to tell us something?" asked Emily.

The cloud shot up and down as though it was nodding its head (clouds are very expressive creatures, you know). Then, in all their confusion, Steven and Emily finally caught sight of the terror that loomed on the ground. You see, a mass of violent wind surrounded the mountain, making its way to the opera house, leaving behind a trail of destruction. Somehow, through the storm, the flowers kept blinking on and off, covering the land in a flashy glow.

"Cloud, take us to the opera house as fast as you can!" shouted Steven. "We must warn everyone before it's too late!" At that, the cloud followed his command and flew them directly to the front door where two silvery-suited footmen greeted them. They both stood tall and confident, completely unaware that a treacherous storm was on its way.

"Are you here for the opera?" asked the footman on the right.

"Well, that was our original intention. We have an opera cake that we must first deliver to Falsetto, though," answered Emily.

"A storm is on its way, you know!" yelled Steven (who was not very good at controlling the volume of his voice in such drastic situations).

The footmen, who thought he was merely offering his opinions on the quality of Falsetto's operas, misunderstood this statement. "I've heard people remark both good and bad things about his operas," said the footman to the left, "but I've never once heard anyone compare them to a storm! What a clever statement. I must remember it." Immediately after speaking, he skipped up the steps and into the opera house, expecting Steven and Emily to follow him. As they entered the entrance hall, they found themselves greeted by rows upon rows of glass cases, each displaying a different costume. "These are terribly valuable," gasped the footman while fixing his gaze on a glistening blue suit. "They are priceless because they are the exact threads and stitches that Falsetto wore during his operas. If you like, I can give you a brief tour."

Steven and Emily shook their head in haste (which, in all honesty, made them rather upset because the costumes looked so lovely behind that shiny glass). Now, these glass cases sat in a way that turned the entire entrance hall into a sort of maze. "Oh, I can never seem to remember my way to the staircase," scoffed the footman. As he turned to face Emily and Steven to apologize, he found himself caught off guard by a bright flash coming from Emily's pocket. "What is causing that blinding flash?" he shouted, causing Emily to remember the flower that Pepper gave her in the museum not so long ago. Immediately, she reached for the tiny tin, and found that the thin petals managed to flicker through the box!

"The storm is closer than ever," she whispered.

Now, at this point, it was quite easy to say that the footman sported the most puzzled look on his face. "You are a peculiar pair. I'm beginning to think that this storm you speak of has nothing at all to do with the opera."

"I'm afraid you're right on both accounts," sighed Emily nervously. "Now, please take us to see Falsetto at once!"

Without saying anything at all, the footman dashed down each aisle until he found the red velvet staircase that would take them directly to Falsetto's room. By the time the three of them reached the third step, they could faintly hear him exercising his voice using various forms of oohs and ahhs. Finally, after running all the way up, they found themselves standing at his door. It was dark blue and covered in glitter, and right above it was a sign that read: PRACTICING GENIUS. DO NOT DISTURB. Nevertheless, they ignored the sign, and pounded on the door until he answered.

"Are you planning on breaking this door to bits?" gasped Falsetto. "If you were, please do it while I'm not around. The suit I am wearing is one of my favorites, and I would certainly hate for it to tear somehow. Now, do you have my opera cake? I absolutely need it if I'm going to calm my stage fright."

Steven and Emily glanced at one another in an attempt to figure out who should break the news of the storm headed their way. Before either of them could say a word, though, Falsetto began to speak, "How horribly odd. I never remember the flowers doing this before," he said of the small flickering bouquet on his table. Each flower in that glass vase flashed relentlessly, just like the flowers in the field and in Emily's pocket.

"They are warning us," crackled Emily. "The flowers are warning us about the storm."

Falsetto paused and blinked his glittery eyes. "What exactly is this storm you speak of, Emily dear?"

Instead of trying to explain everything, which would take far too long in such a dreadful situation, she decided to show him. So, in a rush, she ran to the window and pulled back the heavy curtain, revealing the storm as it approached ever closer to the opera house. "I've spent my entire life trying to forget this sight," cried Falsetto as he gazed outside. "The last time I saw a storm like this was when I was very young. Until this moment, I was certain my memory had forgotten it. Oh, I wish it would have."

"What should we do?" asked Steven from the corner.

Falsetto paced across the room. "Everyone should be seated in the auditorium by now," he said. "Warn them. Warn them even if it means getting on the stage and shouting. They must be warned before the storm hits!"

The footman ran to the doorway. "Follow me and I'll show you the way!" he cried.

"Oh, no you won't!" shouted Falsetto. "You are going to stay with me and help pack up my costumes and baubles so I can move them somewhere safe. Emily and Steven will easily find the auditorium, won't you children?" It was at this moment he realized Emily and Steven had already left, and were halfway to the auditorium.

What a lovely auditorium it was! Everything about it was phenomenal. In fact, it was quite a shame that the winds from the storm would probably destroy most of it. As Emily and Steven rushed down the aisles towards the stage, they heard a shrill, shaky voice calling them from one of the seats. It was none other than Ophelia standing with her opera glasses held firmly to her eyes. "What an odd ensemble for an opera!" she exclaimed. And she wasn't exactly wrong. After all, sand and cookie crumbs clung to the skirt of Emily's (now faded) pink dress. And the shoulders of Steven's blue (and chocolate-stained) suit had tiny holes from the Redbirds' claws. Even still, they could not care less, because things of much more importance stood before them.

"As much as we'd like to continue this conversation," said Steven, "We simply cannot. A storm is on its way, and we need to warn everyone!" They continued to run down the velvety aisles until they finally reached the front of the stage, shouting as they climbed up in an attempt to reach the attention of everyone in the audience.

"Everyone, please listen!" shouted Steven from the center with his arms flailing about. "A windstorm is on its way and we must find a safe place to hide!" His warning must have looked like a performance, because as soon as he spoke, the orchestra played louder and louder until it followed his every move. If he jumped up and down, the music jumped with him. If he shouted and flailed, the symphony followed closely. At that point, their attempt to warn everyone seemed hopeless as ever— that is, until Falsetto appeared majestically from behind the tall, silver curtains. The audience cheered and clapped, only causing more racket.

"How will they ever hear us now?" cried Emily in a state of panic. Through the noise of the music and crowds, they could faintly hear the sound of the wind pressing itself heavily against the walls of the opera house (a sound that only grew louder as the seconds passed).

"No need to worry, dearest Emily!" sang Falsetto in the prettiest tone. "I have a plan." The truth was, though, that he did not have a plan at all. In fact, many things spun around in his mind, and a plan was not even close to being one of them.

225

After a few minutes ticked by without any action on his part, Steven and Emily decided to take matters into their own hands. You see, it was a well-known fact that Falsetto kept a little wedge of opera cake in his suit pocket in case of an emergency. Now, please be aware that the following act might sound quite cruel, but it was the only way to get everyone's attention, and therefore save countless lives. Through the silver haze, Emily marched up to Falsetto, reached for the opera cake, and threw it to the floor as hard as she could, causing a burst of golden dust to fill the air. At that, everything stopped. The orchestra remained silent, and Falsetto hid behind a group of pink ballerinas. In that short moment, the wind howled angrily through the opera house, and a breeze threaded its way through the seats and halls. In a rush, Steven and Emily ran to the front of the stage and shouted as loud as they possibly could.

"There is a windstorm outside, and it is about to hit the opera house. If we start to look for a hiding place now, then we'll all be safe. We cannot waste any time!" Steven warned. Before he advised everyone to leave their seats in an orderly way, though, the audience panicked and ravaged down the rows of the auditorium, causing nothing but confusion and disorder.

As Steven and Emily watched the chaos from the stage, their faces turned bright red with worry. How would they ever get all of those people to safety? In that same moment, Falsetto wondered the same thing. Suddenly, though, a spark of hope filled his mind; he had the perfect plan. In a rush, he left the stage and made his way to the entrance hall. There, he sang as loud as he could, and his voice echoed endlessly against the walls and through the walkways. Like a stampede of sheep, the audience followed his voice, and with his voice, he led them to a secret room that would save them all from even the harshest of winds. From the center of the stage, Steven and Emily watched every last person leave the auditorium.

"Well, he did have a plan after all," sighed Emily with a sense of relief. "We had better follow his voice, too. After all, we wouldn't want to be caught here when the wind—," before she could say another word, the walls cracked as though trying to resist being pushed down. Then, the sound of the wind stopped.

"Emily," whispered Steven. "Take my hand."

"But Steven, I think the storm might have passed! I can barely hear the wind!"

As soon as Emily finished her sentence, the wind ripped through the roof of the opera house, and whipped its pieces all around in circles. At that, Steven yelled as loud as he possibly could, "I'm going to call a cloud! Take my hand at once!"

As soon as Emily's cold little hand trembled to his, he took his golden whistle and made the shrillest of sounds, which beckoned a cloud that looked like it was strong enough to hold a thunderstorm. Once they both managed to climb upon it, the cloud did its best to fly away from the wind. As soon as they flew through the hole in the roof, though, the wind captured the cloud in its tight grip and threw them in circles all throughout the sky!

"Hold on, Emily!" cried Steven as he sat on the cloud with his eyes closed tightly in fear. "I don't know how this is going to end!" he added.

Emily was too stunned to respond, and when she looked to the ground all she could see were miles of trees surrounded by heavy fog (both of which do little to make a fall more comfortable).

"What do you see, Emily?" asked Steven who, in a moment of bravery, glanced at Emily as she lay on the cloud with her eyes peeking over its edge.

Through the wind, she tried to catch her breath enough to answer him, "I see— I only see trees and fog!"

Before she could say another word, the wind ripped the cloud from under them, and they went tumbling straight down towards the forest. At the sight of their falling, the trees took their leafiest branches and prepared to cushion their fall. Just before they hit the ground, the strongest tree in the forest caught them, leaving them practically unscratched without any broken bones to speak of. Before they could even step foot onto the ground, the dark violet sky turned completely black and, like an eruption of lightning, all of the trees flashed in a bright spark. Within seconds, the wind turned into a breeze, and Emily and Steven dazedly rubbed their eyes before they tried to figure out where they landed. The abundance of trees was enough evidence to prove that they were, in fact, in the middle of the forest.

Steven stood, clenching his hands nervously. "I've never been placed in the middle of the forest before. I don't know how to get us out from here." His words sparked a memory within Emily's mind (and perhaps yours, too). Almost immediately, her mind reminded her of a certain map that she and Steven found in Florence and Laurence's chest at the bakery.

"Steven!" she shouted. "Where is the map that leads us to the only hollow tree in Alcovia? The map we found in the bakery?"

Steven reached into his pocket and found the wrinkled map. The first step instructed them to turn left, so they turned left. Then they took twelve steps ahead and stopped. Next, they ran as fast as they possibly could through the forest and turned right three times. Immediately after their third turn, they found the hollow tree facing them and it glowed in the gloomiest shade of gray. Now, just about anyone with a sane mind would blissfully ignore the tree and continue with their day. Emily and Steven were different, though. They were adventurers. So, just like any *proper* adventurers, they crept towards that hollow tree, took each other's hand, and tumbled down, not knowing what they would see next.

Biography

E. S. EDMUNDS
Author

Not unlike the characters in this book, E.S. Edmunds is quite curious. When they aren't writing, they can normally be found doing one of the following things: sipping coffee, people-watching, listening to unpopular songs, or most importantly, gathering details of fantastic events that must be documented.

THROUGH THE VIOLET LIGHT is the debut installation of *THE ODD ADVENTURES OF EMILY AND STEVEN* series. Right now, E.S. Edmunds is collecting the final details of Emily and Steven's most recent adventure, and cannot wait to share the finished story with adventurers everywhere!

⋙❦⋘

S. D. THOMAS
Illustrator

S. D. Thomas is an artist who hails from a sunny valley not far from the ocean. She assists E. S. Edmunds by recording snippets of Emily and Steven's journeys as sketch drawings.

In her spare time, S. D. Thomas enjoys writing stories of her own, playing an antique piano, curling up with her feline companion, and snacking on delicious vegetables.

Made in the USA
San Bernardino, CA
01 December 2018